SURVIVAL GAME
Men of London – Book 9

Susan Mac Nicol

ALSO BY SUSAN MAC NICOL

THE MEN OF LONDON SERIES
Love You Senseless
Sight & Sinners
Suit Yourself
Feat of Clay
Cross to Bare
Flying Solo
Damaged Goods
Hard Climate

THE STARLIGHT SERIES
Cassandra by Starlight
Together in Starlight

OTHER TITLES
Stripped Bare
Saving Alexander
Worth Keeping
Double Alchemy
Double Alchemy: Climax
Love and Punishment
Sight Unseen

www.BOROUGHSPUBLISHINGGROUP.com

PUBLISHER'S NOTE: This is a work of fiction. Names, characters, places and incidents either are the product of the author's imagination or are used fictitiously. Any resemblance to actual events, locales, business establishments or persons, living or dead, is coincidental. Boroughs Publishing Group does not have any control over and does not assume responsibility for author or third-party websites, blogs or critiques or their content.

SURVIVAL GAME
Copyright © 2017 Susan Elaine Mac Nicol

All rights reserved. Unless specifically noted, no part of this publication may be reproduced, scanned, stored in a retrieval system or transmitted in any form or by any means, electronic, mechanical, photocopying, recording, or otherwise, known or hereinafter invented, without the express written permission of Boroughs Publishing Group. The scanning, uploading and distribution of this book via the Internet or by any other means without the permission of Boroughs Publishing Group is illegal and punishable by law. Participation in the piracy of copyrighted materials violates the author's rights.

ISBN 978-1-97596-60-27

There can be no question about to whom this book needs to be dedicated. Having experienced their services firsthand, both for myself and for family members, the paramedics and ambulance drivers out there provide an invaluable service and one that is regrettably paid less than what these amazingly dedicated people are worth. All over the world, we've seen their work firsthand during many recent tragic events, and make no mistake, it's a tough career choice dealing day in and day out with injured, dying and damaged people.

Let's give them their due, not only the ones on the ground but the ones in the air, and if you can spare a few pennies, or your time and involvement, there are great causes to donate to, such as:

theairambulanceservice.org.uk
www.londonambulance.nhs.uk/getting_involved.aspx
www.theasc.org.uk/what-we-do

ACKNOWLEDGMENTS

Bearing the dedication in mind, there is one single person who deserves this acknowledgement for helping this book get written. His name is Binder Smiff (not his real name) and he was an invaluable help to me on giving generously of his time and experiences as a genuine London Ambulance paramedic.

I found Binder when I was looking around the web for a paramedic blog to get some insight on what really goes on out there. I found this one and was hooked:

www.not-on-my-shift.org
Twitter @Binder999

It opened my eyes to everyday life and events in the London streets and made me chuckle more than once. Irreverent, true, blunt and compassionate all in one.

He took time out to write me reams of emails (and boy, they were detailed) on how things get done, to give me the insight I needed and to teach me about the real life out there as a paramedic. While I haven't written overly much about the clinical processes in this story, Binder's help focused me on what NOT to say or assume, and that was just as important.

Read his blog; you won't be disappointed. He recently coined a phrase of his own with respect to his job and remembering the people he's helped, lost, and continues to help while he carries on learning his trade and from his mistakes: *Remember well and never dwell.*

SPECIAL THANKS to my brilliant editor Michelle Klayman at Boroughs. As always, she tells it straight and makes me write a better book. She is my rock.

And to the readers of my books, thank you from the bottom of my heart. Without you, I'd be truly lost. Every one of you is treasured by me, and never doubt it.

SURVIVAL GAME

Chapter One

Some sounds a man never forgets. It could be his newborn child drawing their first breath, or the whispered exhale of a lover as they climax. It could be the first bars of a song at his wedding or a round of applause at his first big casino win.

Some sounds needed to be forgotten. The slap of a fist hitting flesh; the wheeze of breath as ribs shatter; the ringing in the ears from being hit over and over again.

Kyle Tripper wished he could forget the sounds of his past. Hearing them when sleeping was bad enough. He didn't need to be reminded when he was awake.

He sat in the cinema next to Steve, his blind date, hearing him munch through copious amounts of popcorn. On screen, a senseless and violent film played. The bile in Kyle's mouth soured the taste of the sweet Pepsi he'd just sipped.

He held his phone in his lap, trying to make sure its light didn't disturb people behind him as he texted.

This sucks, boss. My date is an arsehole. Making me watch Fistfight instead of Hackaway. FML.

He'd been looking forward to seeing the acclaimed drama about a group of misspent youths taking part in a corporate project to test corporate security.

Ryan Bishop, his friend and employer, was quick to text back.

Hey, Violet, make an excuse and get out of there. Didn't you have to wash your hair?:)

Kyle smirked at the nickname—courtesy of his purple hair and violet contacts—then winced as a man on screen screamed loudly in pain. The plot of *Fistfight* was nothing more than a badly directed effort at giving brawny men the excuse to beat each other senseless. He wasn't a fan. His hands shook a little when he texted his reply.

Yeah, I'm going to bail once we get out of here. He can forget dinner.

In return, Ryan provided a gif of a man running screaming down the street, together with a thumbs-up emoji and the words: **He gives you any trouble, call me. I'll send Mango along to sort him out.** An angry emoji ended the text.

Kyle was sure Ryan's partner would love to sort someone out. Everyone was wary of Mango Munroe and his fierce stare, and even more protective instincts.

Pushing the phone back into his jacket pocket, Kyle heaved a sigh. The one saving grace was that the film was almost over.

Ten minutes later, they were standing in the chilly early March evening air, huffing clouds of steam from cool lips.

"Wasn't that a great film?" Steve enthused as he huddled into his parka. "I love man-on-man fight action and car chases."

Kyle grimaced. "Not my thing," he muttered, shaken and morose from all the gratuitous on-screen violence. "I mean, come on. There's not much to a film like that, is there? Just some guys with their shirts off beating up on other guys." His dark mood deepened. He needed a drink, something to forget the sordid memories the film had stirred.

Steve shoved his arm playfully. "Come on, gorgeous. You mean all that testosterone and chest hair doesn't turn you on just a little bit? Leave you with a need to maybe get up close and personal with someone?"

Steve edged closer, his intent clear.

Kyle didn't want to be there on the street with a man who thought violence was a turn-on. He'd been down that road before. He wanted to go home to his flat a few blocks down from Club Delish—the nightclub where he worked—make hot chocolate, and crawl under a duvet, alone. The contacts in his eyes hurt, making them gritty and sore.

He shook his head, moving out of Steve's orbit. "I'm not feeling too well, actually. I think I'm going to skip your dinner offer and go home."

Steve stared at him, narrowing his eyes. "Honestly? You're going to leave me here with a boner and expect me to take care of it myself? Especially after paying for the film?"

The first trickling of unease danced across Kyle's spine like sly spider legs. He moved further away from Steve, regarding him warily.

"If I'd known the payment for being treated to a movie was taking care of your boner, I'd rather not have gone," he said quietly. "I didn't realise there was a quid pro quo for being company tonight."

My blind date just got fucking worse. Never again.

"Well, that's how the dating world normally works, Kyle." Steve moved closer, anger threading through his tone. Kyle's vision swam as his personal space was encroached. Panic fluttered in his chest, making his heart skip beats.

"Don't crowd me, Steve," Kyle warned. "Can't we just say we didn't agree on the film choice and leave it at that? I don't want to go home on a bad note."

Steve gripped his arm, his mouth twisting in a smirk. "Maybe just a kiss then?" he wheedled, as Kyle's heart thudded madly. "Or a quick blowjob? I bet those beautiful lips of yours know just how to make a man happy. Your lips and my cock—that's a match." Steve leaned in, and instinctively Kyle raised his arm and pushed back on Steve's hard chest.

"N-no," he stuttered. "I'm not kidding. Don't touch me."

Don't touch me, don't touch me, he chanted in his head. *Not with that fire in your eyes and that aggression in your belly. No dark touches, please.*

Kyle wasn't averse to being touched under the right circumstances. What he feared were those touches he thought of as *the dark*. Hardened, insidious fists pummelling into an already aching belly, rough kicks to ribs and face when he was curled up on the floor; pinches to skin already marked with scratches and bruises. Then there were the more intimate ones, the ones Kyle tried not to think about—rough, punitive sex meant to break him.

Steve's hold tightened. "Fuck that," he snarled. "I at least deserve a goodnight kiss."

Kyle was pushed back against the wall and a greedy, wet mouth invaded his own. He tried to keep his lips pressed together, not wanting to give Steve the satisfaction of gaining access. Steve was determined, though, and within seconds a hot, slick tongue was forced into Kyle's mouth.

Please, please, don't do this. Please.

Stomach roiling in fear, he tried again to push Steve away, memories of being forced taking over and blanking out his brain. Bile rose in his throat, and with a touch of hysteria creeping in, he wondered what Steve would do if Kyle vomited into his hungry mouth.

In a weird twist of fate, it was a homophobic bastard walking down the street that saved him from any further mauling.

"Get a fucking room, you faggots," the man yelled.

Steve let go, his lips releasing Kyle's bruised mouth, then he turned and raised a middle finger at the man on the other side of the street. "Fuck you," he yelled. "Fuck off, you wanker."

Kyle seized his opportunity. Within seconds, he was running back down the street as Steve and the Neanderthal traded insults. Kyle's legs pumped like a sprinter's as fear of being caught threatened to overtake him; his deep, rasping breaths were a staccato accompaniment to the sound of his heavy footsteps on the pavement.

His focus was on getting home. Then, maybe, once safe, he could forget about tonight. Forget he'd made another bad decision, that he was a loser when it came to dating.

He thanked God his instinct for self-preservation had included not giving Steve his home address or number.

As Kyle ran past Club Delish, he glimpsed a light on in the flat above the club. Although tempted, he wasn't going to disturb his friends at this hour. Not the best way to pay back Ryan's offering Mango as backup.

When Kyle reached the relative safety of his building, he ran up the stairs to the fourth floor, not even waiting to get the rickety, ancient lift that wheezed from floor to floor as if on its last legs.

It was only when he was at home, locks bolted and security chain slung across the door that he began to relax. He poured himself a favourite drink, a shot glass of white rum, and gulped it back while he waited for his hands to stop shaking.

"Fuck," he swore as he filled the glass again. "I need to stop this blind date shit. It sucks."

He tossed the second shot down then another before he dragged himself into his bedroom. Bed was a good place to be, even though it wasn't even midnight. Being a night owl, used to working 'til the early morning hours, his body clock wouldn't like this early-to-bed scenario.

Well, tonight his body clock could get stuffed. Sometimes knocking yourself out was the only way to forget the past.

Chapter Two

At seven in the morning, Kyle emerged from his bed tired and headachy. Even after three shots of rum, he hadn't slept well. Memories of the past had chased him in his sleep.

Staring at the bathroom mirror, he grimaced at the dark circles under his eyes, which were bloodshot and swollen. He swore softly. No contacts today then. His trademark deep violet would have to be forgotten. Instead, everyone would have to bear the muddy-brown eyes he was born with.

He'd feel naked without his favourite fashion accessory. He didn't need them—he had virtually perfect vision—but liked the cloaking they seemed to afford him. Eyes behind tiny pieces of coloured hydrogel hid emotions he didn't want seen.

He peered closer into the mirror and winced.

Crap. Even guy-liner might be off the cards today. With the amount of rubbing he would no doubt be doing to alleviate his sore eyes, he'd end up looking like a manic panda.

Thank God it was Monday and he had the day off. Not for the first time he was grateful Club Delish was closed Sundays and Mondays.

"Fuck my life," he said gloomily as he stared into the bathroom mirror. "I really thought Steve might be different. But, no. Once again, I go out with an arsehole and once again I end up alone."

My dick really needs to see some action. It's forgotten how to work.

He pulled his boxers away from his hips and stared down at his groin. Yep, his dick was still there, looking sad with only a smidgen of morning wood nestled in a patch of dark bristles. Kyle sighed. He needed to man-scape again but right now, he couldn't be bothered. No one was going to see it anyway.

He brushed his fingers over his nipple rings, hissing at the sensation flooding through him. It was a sorry confession to make, but this action was the closest thing to hands on his body for over a month—well, apart from the occasional jackoff.

"I am so pathetic," he groaned. "Jesus, what I'd give—" He clamped his lips together instinctively at his blasphemy. For a split second, he expected the rolling punch of a fist against his cheek, followed by other things he preferred not to think about.

His gut tightened in both panic and relief. Those days were over; he could say what he liked now, use God, or whomever as many times as he liked without penance. The strange thing was, he hardly ever did. His will had been moulded—no, hammered into submission.

After showering, dressing and savouring a cup of coffee—not pods, his boss Ryan had introduced him to the pleasures of a mouth-watering Italian drip blend—he was ready to face the day. Sitting down on the couch, he looked at his telly viewing options, his mood darkening when he saw the offerings.

He could watch more *Banshee*, but pulled a face as he toyed with the remote. Given his dry spell, he wasn't really in the mood to watch Lucas Hood nail yet another willing lady. The guy had the stamina and sex drive of a rabid rabbit.

He did appreciate the nude scenes, though. Watching Lucas's tight arse pistoning in and out of someone—he tried to ignore the fact he was basically watching soft het porn—led to fantasies that it was his arse Lucas was pounding.

Okay. No telly. Kyle could play cards. Forty Thieves was his patience game of choice. He could practise his shuffling skills, which, he had to say, were awesome, but it was never a bad idea to keep them fresh. The casino he'd worked at mostly had automatic card shufflers to get the job done, but an old and wizened casino dealer had taught Kyle the art of the manual shuffle.

When things had gotten past bad with his ex, Kyle used shuffling to occupy his mind—as long as his fingers hadn't been bruised or cut, or at worst, broken.

No. No cards. Perhaps he could watch *Banshee* and jerk off watching Lucas pound flesh. The very fact he'd considered that idea made him groan loudly.

Fuck, how sad am I?

He contented himself with eating half a tub of Ben and Jerry's Rocky Road ice cream for breakfast because he thought the title suited his life. Then he relented and watched Lucas Hood bang yet another bird, ignoring the twinge of jealousy he felt for the woman.

Bloody hell. That man can sure move his hips.

Two hours later, satiated with a morning wank and feeling sick from the ice cream, he was ready to face the day. He cleaned himself up and threw the now empty ice cream carton in the bin, breathing out a guilty sigh as he did. He checked his phone and was thrilled to find a missed call from his best friend Lucinda Drake, whom he'd last seen over a year ago. He grinned with joy when he heard the message delivered in Luce's nasal New York accent.

"Hey jackass, stop wanking off to hot guys and call me back pronto. I'm back in town unexpectedly and thought we could get together for a late brunch and catch up. Talk ta ya later, London."

Shit, she knows me too damn well.

His spirits rose. It was just like Luce to simply turn up as if no time had passed between them, and surprise him. A late brunch sounded like a plan, perhaps at Jackson and Rye. They made the best avocado Florentine eggs he'd ever tasted. He sighed as he dialled her back.

He couldn't recall a time when Luce hadn't called him London. When they'd worked together at The Bohemian Club in Las Vegas, she'd got this crazy idea that London was the be-all of England. He'd been hard-pressed to tell her that there were other great cities.

Luce answered his return call on the fourth ring. "Hey, London Calling. How you doin'?"

Kyle rolled his eyes, wondering if his profile picture was still the same on Luce's phone. It had been one of him, inebriated after a night out, smiling stupidly next to a red Royal Mail telephone box, with the display name of *London Calling*. They'd both found it doubled-over funny at the time.

"I'm good. Better for knowing you're in town. You didn't give me any warning you were coming over though. Is everything okay?"

He and Luce had worked together for years at The Bohemian Club and become firm friends. Luce still worked there and had a crazy, hectic work schedule that had her travelling around the U.S. to the different casinos that club owned. Her job as a slot operations manager involved a huge amount of what Kyle had thought was boring, mundane work—looking at reports and doing a lot of corporate management stuff involving complex mathematics. He'd rather have poked his eyes out with a stick than do that every day.

She gave a loud laugh. "It was a bit all of a sudden. They offered me a position as VP of gaming, but I like what I do, and I didn't see myself licking ass all day like that job would have required me to. They weren't too happy about it. We had a bit of a spat, and when I said I'd go work for the competition, they quickly backtracked and let me be. Since they were nervous I would bolt, I managed to wangle two months off. I'm pretty beat. They owe me like a year of holiday anyway. I got in two days ago and, obviously, I had to call you once the jet lag settled and I caught up on some sleep. So here I am, London, and I'm all yours."

Kyle chuckled. "Only you could be offered a promotion, turn it down and still end up on the winning team on a two-month timeout abroad."

"Yeah, well," she replied wryly. "I had to see my favourite guy and find out how he's doing. I miss you. Skype and Facebook is fine but it doesn't replace honest to goodness face-to-face contact."

He bit back the lump in his throat. "Yeah, I miss you too."

Luce had been his rock during the turbulent and destructive relationship with his ex-boyfriend, dancer Mario Alves. Not only had she saved Kyle's life, her love and support had been instrumental in helping him out of the abusive relationship he'd seemed mired in. He owed her his sanity.

"So, are we doing this whole brunch thing then?" he teased, already wondering what he should wear and whether he'd be able to manage all the interpersonal contacts he'd encounter when he went out in public. "Is Jackson's okay, say about midday?"

She gave a sultry chuckle. "London, that sounds good to me. I'll see you there. Oh, by the way, look for the chick with blue hair."

She rang off before he could say anything else. He grinned as he put down his phone. She had a thing for changing her hair colour like she did her garish, slogan-inspired tee shirts. The last time he'd seen her she'd been a redhead—as in her hair was fire-engine red. She was a flaming beacon on the casino floor when they'd worked together.

With his mood lightened, Kyle sped into the bathroom, took another shower—because the spunk-smell he sported wasn't quite his cologne of the day choice—and dressed into his favourite pair of Firetrap Blackseal Biker jeans. Teamed with a tight-fitting white tee-shirt under a casual grey chambray long-sleeve shirt, Kyle figured he looked good enough to venture out.

He thought if he didn't drink too much, he might go into the club afterward and finish off a few little jobs he had to do on his list.

He hummed to himself as he picked up his keys, checked he had his wallet and shut the door behind him. The day was suddenly looking a lot brighter.

Chapter Three

Eric Kirby drew a deep, shuddering breath and turned his attention to the unholy mess in front of him. The stench of burnt tyres, blood and fuel pushed at his senses as if to say, "You'd better hurry up. Time is short."

He wanted to snarl that he fucking knew time was short.

Only three months into the year and already I'm wishing for things to get better.

He crouched down under a streetlight and held onto the limp hand of a woman who had whispered her name was Sarah, and who was trapped in the wreckage of what had once been a family sedan. He muttered soothing words to Sarah, whose glazed eyes stared up at him in panic and fear. There was resignation there too.

Damn it. He wasn't going to let that emotion defeat the young woman who lay crushed under a mountain of steel.

The firefighters were on their way; he heard the sirens in the distance.

"Not long now." He smiled reassuringly into Sarah's blue eyes. She stared up at him, a mixture of hope and fear swirling in her gaze. "Can you hear that? It's the fire engine on its way to get you out. You hold on, Sarah. Can you do that for me?"

Sarah's eyes fluttered closed briefly but she nodded. Her hand gripped his tighter. "It's my son's birthday celebration this afternoon," she whispered. "Will I still be able to go?"

He had no doubt this woman wouldn't be going anywhere anytime soon. She had a broken leg, a piece of steel in her side, a badly bruised sternum from the deployed air bag, and she probably had internal injuries he couldn't ascertain.

"How old is he today?" he asked, stroking Sarah's hand softly.

A faint smile lit the pale face of the injured woman. "He'll be twelve. We planned dinner at his favourite restaurant." Tears trickled down her face and her face grimaced in pain. "I'm never going to see him again, am I?"

Eric schooled his face to the comforting look that seemed to help victims. Sarah had lost a lot of blood, and while he'd patched her up as best he could, she needed to go to hospital.

"I've stopped the bleeding for now—and listen." His voice rose as the fire engine came into view, screeching to a halt in front of the mangled metal wreck that had been a VW Passat. "Here are the firemen. They'll get you out, and then we'll check you again and get you to the hospital. They'll call your family and let them know what happened. I'm sure you'll be seeing your son in no time at all."

He made to stand up, to get out the way for the firemen to do their job, and Sarah's eyes widened.

"Don't leave me please," she begged. Her fingers held onto his tightly.

Eric motioned towards the men coming his way then bent to speak to Sarah. "I need to get out of the way, let the other guys do their job." The firemen were there now, waiting expectantly, armed with the tools of their trade. "I won't be far. You'll be fine in their hands. I'll see you afterward, and I'll get you all prepped up for the ambulance ride, 'kay?"

He stood up and met the eyes of his crewmate, Aaron, who regarded him with compassion as he mouthed, "You got this one, partner."

Eric nodded tiredly and moved out the way as he turned his hand to its side to smooth hair away from his sweaty, grimy forehead. His neoprene gloves were coated with blood from where he'd tried to staunch the bleeding from pieces of steel embedded in his patient's side and leg. He peeled the gloves off and threw them into the disposal bin in the back of the ambulance.

I'm not sure how much longer I can do this.

Aaron patted him on the shoulder. "Looks like they're getting her out okay," he muttered as they watched the firemen at work. Aaron's round face was weary, dirt coating his forehead and cheeks. He ran a hand through his bristled dark hair. "Poor woman's having a fucking rough day. That arsehole who sideswiped her ought to be locked up." He scowled at the man sitting pale and dejected on the side of the road, surrounded by medical personnel and police alike.

"According to eyewitnesses, the guy was on his phone and didn't see the traffic light was red. Damn, I wish people would understand that it's times like these"—Aaron waved a hand at the scene playing out before them—"that just brings home the whole 'don't check your mobile phone when you're driving because you could kill someone' warnings."

Eric nodded in agreement. "Yep. It's just not worth it." He rubbed his eyes, sudden fatigue stealing through him. "Hopefully the fire department won't be too long getting her out." He squinted through tired eyes at the firemen as the car door pulled away with a screech of metal. He shuddered. He'd never get used to hearing that sound. It went right through him.

Aaron sighed heavily. "No problem. I'm going to check the truck again, see that everything's good for her ride to the hospital. I'll be with you in a sec to load our patient onto the stretcher." He left Eric standing there, watching as the firemen secured the vehicle. After what seemed like a lifetime, one of them raised a hand and waved Eric over.

"She's good to go," the blond-haired guy called out.

Any other time, Eric might have quite fancied getting down and dirty with him. The guy was a cutie. But now, covered once again with someone else's blood, tired to his core and wanting nothing more than to finish the hell-shift and get home to slouch on the couch, he didn't have the energy to worry about what his dick might think.

Before long, his patient was prepped, ready to be taken to the hospital. Together he and Aaron loaded the now semi-conscious woman into the ambulance. Within minutes, Aaron at the wheel, and Eric in the back with their patient, they were speeding their way to the nearest Accident and Emergency centre.

After wheeling Sarah into the A and E ward, and assuring her she was in good hands, they cleaned up the truck as best as they could before the next call out.

There was a young woman who vomited her guts up from drinking too much. Next was an old man suffering from stomach gas who thought it was a heart attack.

Shift finally over, Eric and Aaron travelled back to the Shoreditch station. Both paramedics were permanently stationed there, called having a "line," which was highly sought after. Eric was pleased he and Aaron didn't have to move between stations anymore.

"Can I just say I'm glad you were the attending on this one?" Aaron said with a grimace. "I couldn't face paperwork and reports right now. Honest, I'm so damn tired I couldn't even find my dick to pee."

Eric laughed tiredly. "Me too. I hate paperwork, but some poor sap's got to do it."

"I'll stay and help you if you want, after we clean the truck up." Aaron's grudging response made Eric smile. He knew if he accepted the offer, Aaron would stay. But Aaron had other responsibilities.

"Nah, you get off. Your grandma will be looking forward to seeing you. God forbid I
should detain you from your regular dinner visit. She'll circumcise me herself."

Aaron laughed loudly. "Now there's a thought." He visited his grandmother often to check on her health, often with Eric in tow. He liked Aaron's spitfire of a grandmother, and the feeling was mutual.

"She'll probably force-feed you matzo ball soup and freshly made challah." Eric's mouth watered at the thought of food prepared by Aaron's bubbie, Norma. Eric had eaten there many a time, enjoying the warm yet biting sarcasm of the spry seventy-five-year-old.

With his own family living in another county, he loved the old woman as much as Aaron did. And despite Norma's overprotectiveness and constant belabouring to bring a young man round to meet her, she felt the same about him.

"Yeah, in between her telling me to find a good Jewish woman and settle down to give her great-grandkids," Aaron grumbled as he navigated into the parking garage.

Eric chuckled and they fell silent as they parked the truck. *At least we don't have to restock*, he thought tiredly.

There was a company that came in to replenish the vehicle with what the next team would need for the following shift.

He backslapped an exhausted Aaron. "Come on. Let's get Betty cleaned up and then we can blow this joint."

Betty was the affectionate name for any truck they manned, named after Betty Rizzo from Grease, whom Aaron adored. Eric had been more into Danny himself.

Aaron grinned. "Yeah, let's do it." He looked at his watch. "Shit, it's eight am. A twelve—make that thirteen—hour shift never seemed so long. Thank God we're both off now for a couple of days." He patted Eric on the back.

"Grab your mop, partner. I'll get the bucket."

An hour later, the two tired men laid down their gear and smiled at each other in exhaustion.

"See you in forty-eight hours, buddy." Aaron rolled what were obviously aching shoulders. "I think I might just sleep it away."

"See you, mate. Enjoy your time off." Eric gave Aaron a bro hug then watched him walk away. He heaved a deep sigh and walked into the small, crowded office to finish his paperwork. He thought sleeping in most of today had a good ring to it. Then perhaps later tonight he'd go by and see if his friend Ryan Bishop wanted to go for a drink.

Truth be told, Ryan hadn't been looking so good lately. Normally a bundle of energy, the man seemed to have something on his mind. Perhaps tonight might be the night Eric got to drag it out of him.

He grinned to himself as he powered up the computer. Of course, if Ryan's partner Mango was back in town from eco-warrioring, Eric might not be welcomed. Mango had a streak of jealousy a mile long when it came to him. It was no doubt a remnant of the days Eric and Ryan had tried dating but it hadn't worked out. Ryan had still been too crazy in love with his burly eco-warrior.

Still, there was a silver lining. Perhaps that cute, sexy manager at the club, Kyle, would be there tonight.

The last time Eric had seen Kyle, he'd seemed quite taken with him as well. The young man's beautifully coloured eyes had drifted over in his direction more than once during the conversation.

"Unfortunately, assuming he is gay and interested, a paramedic and a nightclub manager isn't the best match," Eric muttered to himself as he titled his head from side to side, trying to ease the kinks out of his neck. "Chances are we'd never get any time together with the hours we work. Fucking government cutbacks."

He finished his report and powered down the computer. Time to go home, sleep, and then see what the night brought. Assuming when he woke up he still had the energy.

Chapter Four

"Sooo…" Lucinda Drake reached over and stole the last two remaining scallops from Kyle's plate. His indignant "Oi" didn't seem to hold much sway as she popped them both into her mouth. "No new beau on the scene then? No sexy piece of ass in the picture?"

He snorted as he picked around the remaining lettuce on his plate. "Not bloody likely. The blind date I had last night turned out to be a real creep. I have this knack of choosing the wrong people." He didn't want to tell the full extent of what had happened or he'd be subjected to Luce's sympathies and probably be hauled in between scented lady bosoms.

She ran a perfectly manicured hand through her hair. The polished red tips clashed with the strands of bright electric-blue hair that swung down to her shoulders. "Baby, don't say that. You'll find the right guy one day. Just have to pick the truffles out of the pig swill first."

He made a face. "Ugh. Way to go with that analogy. I feel sick right now."

He knew he wasn't the most discerning of people when it came to relationships—thoughts of his ex sent cold chills through him—but surely, he had to get a break sometime.

He wanted to find a man who was warm and funny, and didn't use his fists as a solution to everything. Someone who wouldn't break Kyle and leave him bleeding and ashamed on the floor.

His insides churned and he closed his eyes, thankful that piece of his life was over.

"London? You okay?" Lucinda reached over and covered his hand with her own. "Your hands are freezing. Where did you go right then, or don't I want to know?"

He blinked. "I just closed my eyes for a second."

Lucinda's compassionate gaze washed over him. "You were gone almost a minute; you didn't hear a word I said." Her stare darkened. "London, you have to talk to someone about this. God knows it's been a long time but it's obvious you're still stressing about it. You told me you were going to see someone."

Shit. Here come the bosoms.

His defences went up like solid steel gates. He picked his napkin off his lap and wiped his mouth. "Luce, I told you, I'm fine. I don't need a therapist."

I don't need to relive my life as a puppet, telling some stranger I was a willing, idiotic marionette who didn't have the guts to leave a psychopath. I don't need anyone else knowing how spineless I was.

She leaned back, green eyes sparking emerald fire. "I know you think you deserved it, that you were gutless, but that's not true. People with abusive partners get into this rut—"

He threw down his fancy napkin. "Can we leave this alone please? You didn't come five thousand miles to rehash my past. I want to have fun while you're here, not be browbeaten into submission." He chanced a weak grin. "Been there, done that."

Lucinda gazed at him then exhaled and nodded. "Fine. You want to move onto more sappy subjects, how's that boss of yours? And the nightclub? You still enjoying it there?"

He nodded, grateful to be back to less hurtful memories. "I love it. It's hard work, long hours, and you need the patience of a saint, but it's great. Ryan is a cool boss, his partner Mango is scary on the outside but a kitten at heart, and I get to run the club the way I see fit when Ryan isn't there. Which isn't often. The man's a sucker for work."

"Have you met anyone you'd be interested in working there?" Lucinda asked curiously. "I mean it is a gay club."

Kyle remembered a man dressed in a paramedic's uniform with bright green eyes, chestnut hair and brawny arms. "There was this hunky guy I met a while ago called Eric. He's a paramedic who attended a heart attack incident we had in the club. He's a friend of Ryan's. I think they dated once but it didn't work out."

"And? You interested in him?" Lucinda leaned forward, eyes bright with interest.

He shrugged. "I don't really know that much about him. We didn't get much time to talk when he was there last. He was on his way out with Ryan. He's really yummy though."

And how he'd envied Ryan that night he spent with Eric. He'd seemed like a truly nice bloke.

"So call him. Ask him out. What have you got to lose?" She motioned the waiter over to bring the bill. "Grab that bull by the horns, babe. Maybe we can double date and I can find a nice girl to bring with me. We can hang out, shoot the breeze and have some fun together."

He took the bill the waiter had brought over, only to have it plucked from his hands by scarlet-tipped fingers.

"Mine," she said with a steely eyed glare. "You don't get to pay this one. Don't even argue or I'll shove a Tampax down your throat."

He gaped. "What? That's disgusting. Why would you even say something like that to me in public?"

She gave a wicked grin. "Because talking about lady things was always one way to shut you up. Remember that time we got stoned and we had a whole discussion about vaginas and what we lesbians like to call them? I think the best one was bearded—"

He hurried to press his finger to Lucinda's wicked mouth. "Please, don't say it. You can pay the damn bill."

She smirked and opened her purse to take out her credit card. "You can leave the tip if you like. Don't think I didn't notice you ogling that waiter's groin earlier. He certainly wears tight well. I could see every cock ridge he had to offer."

Kyle groaned. "Dear God, can you keep quiet for a minute before they kick us out of here for all the sex speak?"

She waggled her eyebrows at him. "Then we get to not pay the bill. Win-win all the way."

The bill was duly paid—he winced at the price of a fancy lunch for two in a Covent Garden restaurant—and before long they were standing on the pavement in the cool evening air.

Lucinda wrapped her bright green faux-fur parka around her. "So, what are your plans for tonight then? I'm going over to see my sister and her kids in Edgeware. You're welcome to come along."

He tried to hold back his horror at that suggestion. Lucinda's sister Maggie was a brash, noisy woman with a heart of gold and three rambunctious and rowdy spoilt children. He'd only visited them once before and that had been enough.

"No, sorry, can't make it. I'm going into work to finish off some chores. It'll give me a head start tomorrow—we have a fancy function on at lunchtime. I'll take a rain check."

Lucinda pounced on him and, as expected, he was smothered with warm, female flesh under silk.

"Great to see you, London. We're gonna be doing this bonding thing a lot while I'm here." She released him and he found he could now breathe.

"Sounds good to me. Thanks for lunch. I'll give you a call tomorrow and we can set up another date? Maybe we can go to a West End show. I know you always wanted to see *Wicked*. Perhaps Ryan can get us some cheap tickets. He's got connections in the theatre business."

Her eyes lit up. "Oh yeah, that would be awesome. I'd love to see that show. Call me tomorrow then and let me know what's happening. Lovely to see you, babe. Love you loads, you know that."

She planted a perfumed kiss on his cheek then left with a waft of expensive scent. She clambered into her taxi and Kyle waved as it sped off.

He looked at his watch. Time to do a little work then figure out what he was going to do for the rest of the night.

It was around six pm when Kyle let himself into the club. He shook his head when he saw the light burning under Ryan's door. His boss always seemed to be working, even when the club was closed.

He huffed. *He* couldn't talk, being here on his day off too.

Bloody hell, we're both losers.

"Boss?" He knocked on Ryan's door, waited a while then tapped again. Sounds emanated from inside the room, so he knew someone was there. He opened the door and walked in. "I thought I'd come in, do the line cleaning, stock some barrels and get everything ready for—"

He stopped short at seeing Ryan on his knees, enthusiastically blowing Mango, who leaned back against the desk with a beatific look upon his face.

Oh shit, I take back my thought about Ryan being a loser.

Suppressing his laughter, Kyle backed out of the door. Maybe they hadn't noticed him.

"What the fuck?" Mango snarled, his voice strangled. "Ry, you in the habit of just letting anyone walk into your office like that? What the hell happened to knocking first?"

He hauled his lover to his feet and then tucked himself away, his face red. Ryan licked his lips and smirked at Kyle.

"Well, hello there," he murmured. "This is a surprise."

"I did knock," Kyle said, trying to keep his amusement at bay. "Twice. Obviously the two of you were preoccupied."

"Yeah, and the club is closed, so no one should be here." Mango hauled his arse up onto the desk. "Ry, talk to your staff," Mango whined. "Tell them they can't just barge in when you and I are having our happy times."

Kyle broke into chuckles at Mango's petulant tone. "Sorry. I didn't mean to *barge* in."

Ryan sauntered over to him looking like a cat who'd got the cream. Kyle was sure he'd interrupted them before *that* happened though. "Ignore Grumpy Puss over there. He's just mad he didn't get to finish. I'll help him out with it in a moment. So, you managed to ditch that douche of a date last night then?"

Kyle couldn't help shuddering. "Yeah, I did. Won't be seeing him again."

Ryan's eyes softened. "You seem out of sorts about it. Anything I need to know?" His tone had an edge to it and Kyle had no doubt that if he so wanted, Ryan and Mango would deal further with the unpleasant Steve.

"No, I left him there, went home and crawled into bed. Nothing to report, boss."

"Hmm." Ryan didn't seem convinced. "Okay. What are you doing here now?"

"I just finished having a late lunch with Luce and rather than go home and eat ice cream again and watch other people getting off on telly, I thought I'd come by here and finish up a few things." He snorted. "I didn't expect to find a free porn show."

Mango raised his middle finger at him but grinned as he did so. Kyle had always found Mango's bark to be far worse than his bite, despite his carefully crafted reputation meant to scare people shitless.

Ever since Ryan had face-planted in the club a while ago, Mango had been a mother hen where Ryan was concerned.

Ryan frowned. "It's your day off, sweetz. You should be out there having fun, not stuck here working." He gave a wicked smile at Mango. "At least I was having fun even though I'm here. My boyfriend here decided he fancied a bit of boss-employee roleplay so we—"

Mango's face flushed. "Okay, Ry, way to tell the world about our sex life. Could we not do that please?" He squirmed uncomfortably.

Ryan chuckled and pressed a kiss to his cheek. "Such a shy boy, aren't you?" He batted his eyelashes. "Well, I know I'm new here, sir, so I don't like to presume, but could I please suck your cock again now? Mr Tripper was just leaving."

"Fuck, Ry…you are so bad." Mango's tone was husky and needy. He looked across at Kyle who was slowly backing out of the office.

"I'm going," he murmured. "You two have fun. See you tomorrow. Remember to breathe, boss." He winked at Mango saucily. He was waved out impatiently as Ryan got busy unbuttoning his lover's Levi's.

Kyle closed the door behind him and stood shaking with laughter—laughter tinged with a little envy and a lot of yearning. The pair had been through some turbulent times recently, what with Ryan breaking up with Mango then taking him back. But they appeared to be stronger than ever and it was clear to see the two men were besotted with each other.

I want that. I want someone to come home to who isn't going to make me lose my breath in fear. Someone who won't treat me like a personal punching bag.

Thoughts of his ex-boyfriend caused his heart to sputter even though the man was thousands of miles away. All Kyle had to see nowadays was the physique of a six-foot, black-haired and muscled man to send chills down his spine.

He was making a last-minute check that he'd put everything away when he felt the presence of someone behind him. An unknown man's cologne teased his nostrils. Heart hammering, Kyle turned swiftly, stepping back defensively. His movement triggered a pile of toilet rolls to go tumbling from the bar countertop to the floor. He'd been about to put them in the gents' loo before he left.

Kyle met the startled gaze of pale jade-green eyes in a tanned complexion, surrounded by short, deep auburn curls. Eric Kirby towered over Kyle by at least six inches and he felt intimidated by the broad shoulders and powerful body.

"Kyle? You okay? You've gone horribly pale." Eric moved toward Kyle, who stepped back again as he tried to get his panic under control.

"Hi, Eric—you surprised me, that's all. I was expecting anyone else. I mean, I'm just putting these away." He waved at the toilet rolls spread across the floor. "I'll pick them up now. No, don't you do it, it was my mistake…"

God, he has beautiful lips. I'd really like to kiss them one day.

"Don't be daft," Eric said, still seeming a little wary of Kyle's overreaction. "I'm sorry I scared you. The door was open and I saw you there, so thought I'd come on over and say hi before I went to see Ryan."

Kyle's gut churned. "You said the door was open? I thought I'd locked it." His hands shook as he piled another roll on the top of a growing mound. He bent down and picked up two errant toilet rolls and put them back on the bar counter.

Eric shook his head as he placed the last straggler on the top of the pile of pink rolls. "No, the keys were still in the lock too. I took them out." He handed over a set of keys. "Here you go."

Kyle stared down at them in bemusement. "I've never done that before. I always make sure I lock the door when we're alone in here and the club's shut. Shit."

Anyone could have walked in. Apparently last night's episode with Steve left me more rattled than I thought.

"Not a big deal. It's all good now." Eric cast a worried glance in Kyle's direction. "Are you sure you're feeling all right?"

"Yeah, I'm good. Thanks." He managed a smile. "Um, about seeing Ryan. I wouldn't go in there right now. He and Mango are kind of in the middle of something. I already interrupted them. I don't think they'd take kindly to another intrusion."

"Ah." Eric's grin lightened the room. "I get it. Well, I only came by to ask him if he wanted to go for a drink. If Mango's here, I guess they'll be busy for a while. Guess I should go then." Sighing, he turned to leave.

Kyle's spirits dropped. He could have done with a bit of a natter but he didn't want to risk Eric giving him the brush off.

With a deep breath, Kyle plastered a false smile on his face just as Eric turned around with a question in his green eyes.

"If you're on your own right now, perhaps you fancy coming for a drink with me?" Eric tilted his head. "There's a great little pub down the road called The Griffith. They make a mean plate of chips with an ale."

Kyle's smile went from false to real in a split second. "Really? Yeah, I guess I could—just wait a sec, will you? I need to put these away in the loo then I'll get my stuff and we can go."

Better freshen up first.

Kyle picked up the toilet roll pile and with arms full, he manoeuvred his way to the bathroom. He'd need to check on the special Deep Purple cloakroom to tidy up, but that could wait.

Once inside the loo, he dumped the supplies in the closet, ensured there was paper in each cubicle, and then retrieved his freshen-up kit from the locked medicine cabinet. He took out his toothbrush and toothpaste, cologne and antiperspirant, scrubbed his teeth 'til they gleamed and made lavish use of the toiletries before stuffing them back in the cabinet.

When he got to the front of the club Eric stood at the front desk, seemingly engrossed in a magazine. Kyle watched as Eric's large, blunt fingers flicked the papers.

Hmm, big hands…

Kyle smirked. In truth, he thought that to be an urban legend. He'd met guys with tiny hands and huge dicks, and guys with big hands, but you'd need an eyeglass to see what nestled between their legs. In Vegas, he'd even met a guy with three balls. One dick, unfortunately.

He cleared his throat and Eric turned around. His face lit up. "You ready to go, then?" He put the magazine down and grinned. "It's only five minutes down the street."

Kyle nodded as he collected his satchel and slid his arms into his faux Hugo Boss padded hoodie.

"That's fine. I could do with the exercise."

"You don't look like you need exercise," Eric murmured. "You look pretty fit to me."

Oh, he was flirting now, was he? This evening promised to be enjoyable.

The walk didn't take long and while they didn't say much weaving through streets teeming with people, it was a companionable silence. Before long they were settled in a quiet corner of the pub, enjoying the local ale.

Kyle may have been a top-notch mixologist and sought-after casino host in Vegas, but at heart he was a simple soul with a love for good beer and rum.

Eric sat back, legs akimbo, beer in hand and regarded Kyle lazily. "So, Ryan and Mango were getting it on when you walked in on them then?"

Kyle laughed. "Yep. Ry was delivering what looked like one helluva blowjob and Mango looked as if he wanted to deck me for interrupting."

Both men chuckled and took a sip of their drinks. Kyle looked at Eric questioningly. "So, tell me if I'm overstepping the mark. You and Ryan tried dating but it didn't work out? What happened?"

Eric shrugged, his long fingers wrapping around his beer bottle as he gestured toward Kyle. "Oh, you know. We thought there were sparks, but there weren't, and it turned out we were better off as friends. Ryan hadn't got over Mango, and, frankly, I thought it was a matter of time until they found their way back together." He grinned. "I'm glad I was right. Those guys deserve each other."

Kyle raised his bottle in a salute. "Amen to that."

He couldn't help noticing the line of Eric's throat as he drank. There was a certain spot—just there—that begged to be licked. Kyle saw himself leaning over the table and dragging his tongue up the stubbled throat then finding Eric's plump lips in a kiss that—

"Earth to Kyle." Eric regarded him with amusement. "Do I have something on my face?"

The warm flush that suffused Kyle wrapped around his body. "Erm, no, sorry. I was thinking of something else."

Eric raised an eyebrow, which Kyle found mouth-wateringly sexy. "Anything I should know about? I almost felt like you were getting ready to serve me up with a slice of lemon and eat me."

Kyle couldn't resist it. "I'd love to eat you," he murmured. "It's one of my favourite things to do."

Eric's eyes widened, and the look of lust that overtook his face left Kyle breathless.

"Oh yeah?" Eric shifted in his seat. "We'll have to try that one night. Now that you've offered, you can't take it back." He grinned and settled back in his chair. "I'm sure I could return the favour." His gaze smouldered as he stared into Kyle's eyes.

Kyle's arse clenched at the thought of Eric's tongue licking his hole, getting deep inside him. His cock was enjoying the idea too.

They were interrupted by their waitress, which probably was just as well. Kyle was sporting a hard-on that threatened to blow. She plunked down their plates of chips, asked if they wanted anything else, barely waited for their head-shakes, and then left.

Kyle lathered his in brown sauce, ignoring Eric's grimace, then popped a hot chip in his mouth and gave a deep groan. "Oh, that tastes good." He licked the sauce off his fingers, while watching Eric's face.

Eric shook his head, and gave a soft laugh. "I see what you're trying to do," he muttered. "God, you are such a tease."

Kyle smirked. "Well, thank you, kind sir. I do try."

Their conversation turned to football, politics and some animated discussion about who was the best James Bond when Eric asked a question that Kyle wasn't ready to answer.

"So, Ryan tells me you used to work in Vegas as a croupier? Must have been fantastic. Sounds glamorous. What made you come back to the UK?" His head was cocked to one side and his expression was one of true curiosity.

Shit, Eric, did you have to go there now? We were having such a good time.

Kyle gulped down the rest of his almost finished drink then shrugged. "I got tired of it all. It's a cutthroat business, and believe me, it looks like a beautiful lifestyle on the outside, but inside it's dirty as hell. Not everything shiny is good; sometimes it's just the dark tarnish that makes it look so inviting."

Especially when that dark tarnish is your ex-boyfriend.

Eric huffed. "Wow, profound. I get where you're coming from. Sometimes people say things like, 'It must feel wonderful saving people in your job.'" His tone was laced with bitterness, face shadowed, and for the first time, Kyle got a glimpse that there were demons lurking within Eric Kirby. "It's the *not* saving people that churns your gut and gives you nightmares." He looked at his plate for a moment then lifted his head with a strained smile. "Sorry. Didn't mean to put a downer on the evening."

Kyle waved a hand. "No problemo. We all have our crosses to bear." He reached around into his jacket pocket. "I did learn a few parlour tricks over there, though. Wanna see a card trick?"

Want misdirection at its best, and a great subject-changer? Always have a deck of cards in your pocket.

Eric nodded eagerly, the shadows disappearing from his eyes. "Fuck, yes. I love card games and tricks. There was this old geezer who used to sit outside the station house in Shoreditch where I work, and he could do this crazy thing with an egg and a pack of cards."

Kyle laughed. "Sounds fun. Mine doesn't have an egg but I hope you'll enjoy it anyway." He winked at Eric.

This would be fun.

As a casino dealer working in Vegas, he'd learnt a few tricks. At any given moment, he'd been expected to deal, pitch cards, move chips, sweep cards, check the players weren't cheating and pay out to the punters. Impressing Eric would be easy.

He started with a couple of easy tricks, like producing a royal flush one after the other.

Eric's eyes boggled. "How the hell do you do that? I thought the odds of dealing one of those was astronomical."

Kyle chuckled as Eric stared at him with disbelief. As did the few fascinated onlookers who watched avidly.

"The probability of receiving a royal flush is slim. I could deal twenty hands of poker every night of the year, and in eight to nine years you would hit one royal flush in the deal." He grinned wickedly. "It's all in the sleight of hands and making the audience focus elsewhere. We call it card manipulation. Here, look at this."

Deftly, he shuffled the deck of cards and dealt four onto the table. With a flip of his wrist, he turned each one over. Eric watched, mouth open, as Kyle revealed four aces. Then he gathered the cards together, shuffled and did it again.

During the parlour tricks, they'd both had a couple more drinks—bought by the clapping onlookers who were enjoying the show—and were fairly buzzed.

Kyle began a running commentary on the card facts he'd learnt over the years.

"Ever notice how the ace of spades always stands out in a deck of cards? There's a reason for that. Once European leaders saw that playing cards had become so popular, they decided there was an opportunity to levy taxes on a deck of cards. Typical, right? Levy tax on a game people enjoy." Kyle waved a hand airily. "The leeches put a stamp on the wrappings of playing cards. Of course, the wrappings got discarded, so to make certain the tax stuck, they decided to stamp one card in a deck to indicate the duty had been paid. In the eighteenth century, the ace of spades commonly received the stamp, probably because it lay on the top of every deck."

"Wow, that's fascinating." Eric watched as Kyle laid out a perfect arc of cards on the table. "You never think about cards having history."

Kyle nodded. "Most playing cards have a story behind them. The king of hearts was fashioned after King Charlemagne, the first Holy Roman Emperor. He was born around seven-forty-two and is the only king in the deck without a moustache, and he has a sword through his head. They used to call him the 'Suicide King.'"

"But how, I mean, you guessed every card I chose, and that thing you do with the royal flush, how do you even...?" Eric's voice trailed off in awe and Kyle basked in the pleasure of it.

"Oh, it's easy when you know how," he sniffed as he shuffled the deck adeptly, loving how it made Eric catch his breath. Practice made perfect after all. "It's all about speed, reading people, misdirection and having fingers the speed of light." He shuffled the cards dexterously then fanned the pile on the table.

Eric nudged his shoulder. "Show off," he muttered. "Do your cocktails taste as good as your mad card skills play?"

Imbued with a sense of confidence that he'd impressed Eric, Kyle threw caution to the wind and decided the flirting could escalate a little.

"Oh, my cock tastes just fine," he murmured, rejoicing at the sight of Eric's face pinking up and his eyes darkening. "Oh, *cocktails*, sorry, I must have misheard you."

If *that* didn't indicate he was interested in the gorgeous man sitting across from him with hunger in his eyes, with lips that were meant to be invaded by Kyle's tongue, then Eric was not the man Kyle thought he was.

Eric leaned over and brushed his fingers over Kyle's eyebrow piercing. It was new, to match the one in his left ear. He'd got rid of the nose piercing a while ago, deciding it was too much.

The feel of calloused fingers on his mouth made Kyle shiver with delight as his cock hardened in his jeans.

"Have you ever had a lip piercing or a tongue stud?" Eric asked as he slid his finger along Kyle's bare lip, gathering up the moisture there.

Kyle swallowed, his cock deflating, cold chills making a slow path down his spine. The memory of Mario trying to rip out Kyle's tongue piercing with his teeth played behind his eyes and he could hear. Mario's disgusted voice as if he were here in the room with them.

Wanton slut. You're a perversion in the sight of God. You tempt me and that's a sin.

"No," Kyle managed to say, as the images and sounds flickered in his head. "Not anymore."

Lip and tongue piercings are too easy to rip out, leaving shredded flesh behind.

Kyle moved back, away from Eric's fingers.

Disappointment and concern registered on Eric's face. "Hey, I hope I didn't step over any line," Eric sat back and drained his drink. "I don't want to spoil what's been a great night."

Kyle shuffled the deck, tidied them up and put them back in the box. He slipped his deck into his jacket pocket.

"It's not you. I just…have…some issues. I'm trying to leave them behind where they belong, but sometimes, it's not so easy, you know?"

Eric sighed heavily. "Looks like we both have our demons." He glanced at his watch, which was a big, masculine timepiece that suited his thick wrist. "It's late anyway. I should be going." He stood up and collected his sheepswool jacket from the back of the chair.

"Sorry," Kyle said wearily. "Way to end an evening." He stayed seated, looking down at the table, wondering whether he should have another drink before going home to his empty flat.

He was surprised when warm hands cupped his chin and forced his eyes upward. Eric regarded him with warmth and compassion. "Don't be sorry. I had fun." White teeth flashed then vanished. "I'm off again tomorrow then back to the grindstone. Shift work is a bit of a bitch to make social arrangements around, but I hope we can make some time to do this again. I know the nightclub life isn't conducive to the normal social thing either."

Kyle stood, having decided against a drink. "I get Sunday and Mondays off, and start work at three in the afternoon generally until close, which is around two am. Ryan's pretty chilled about working hours though. He's a great believer in the flexi-time approach." He pulled a small, tattered card out of his jeans pocket. "Here's a Club Delish card—it has my direct work number on it."

Kyle didn't give out his mobile number to anyone he hadn't known *forever*. He liked Eric but it was too early still to trust the man with something that personal.

"Excellent." Eric shrugged into his coat. "Here's my mobile number. Feel free to text me if you get some spare time." Obviously, Eric didn't suffer from the same reservations.

Kyle nodded. "Sure, will do. Thanks again for the company."

"Anytime." There was an awkward silence then Eric gestured toward the door. "I guess I should say cheerio and get off then."

"What, here? You have a kink for doing it in public?" Kyle was feeling better at the idea he hadn't been written off as being a loser.

"Well, that's for me to know and you to find out." Eric winked.

Kyle watched with a smile as Eric walked out of the pub.

Chapter Five

Walking down to the tube station, Eric felt what he'd said had somehow upset the balance of the relationship between him and Kyle. Well, not quite a relationship—he supposed he couldn't call it that after a couple of chance meetings and one night of drinks together. He certainly wanted to get to know Kyle better. The man was entertaining, sexy as hell with his lithe body, piercings and that eye-catching purple-black hair.

After Eric had brought up the tongue-piercing thing, Kyle had switched off and disappeared into himself. Some old memory had really rattled him.

Eric's mobile rung, and when he saw who it was, his mood lifted.

Deacon.

"Dekes, my man. What's happening? Chrissy kick you out and you need a place to stay for the night?"

His best friend's laugh echoed down the line. "Naw. You know my wife loves me too much to do that. She couldn't live without my hot, sexy bod in her bed for one night, could you, sweetheart?" There was the sound of a scuffle then Chrissy's laughter sounded in Eric's ear.

"Hey, Eric, don't listen to a word my husband says. And when he tells you why he's calling, please tell him no, like you usually do. The survival of our future child depends on it."

Deacon came back on the line sounding put out. "She has no faith in me, that woman. None at all."

Eric chuckled as he leaned against the wall of the tube station. "That's because she knows you. What hare-brained scheme have you found for us to invest in now?"

Deacon was an inveterate believer in weird and wonderful business ventures they could get involved in. The man was a dreamer and an idealist, the thing most people who knew him loved about him. One thing he was not, however, was able to realise when something novel or faddy was a bad idea. He was a successful garden designer in Torquay with green fingers and a top-notch clientele, so his business acumen was impressive.

Deacon ploughed on, enthusiasm growing as he spoke. "I was talking to a lady who has this magnificent greenhouse growing cucumbers. We got around to talking about how much waste there was when you slice the end of a cucumber and then it goes all soggy and you have to throw the whole thing away."

Standing there watching the stream of commuters on the London streets, Eric began to laugh, quietly so as not to offend his friend. He had a feeling he knew where this was going.

"So, I thought about making a cucumber topper, like a clip you could put on the end over the sliced part, to keep it fresh. You could even make them into all sorts of shapes, like cartoon characters, flowers, Christmas themed, that sort of thing. Chrissy thinks I'm crazy but I think it could be a really good idea."

Eric tried to muffle his amusement when he replied. "Well, sounds interesting. Except I'm sure someone tried pitching that on *Dragon's Den* and got laughed out of town. Something about, 'Why would someone buy that when all they need is a bit of tin foil or cling film to wrap around it? Or a plastic salad crisper.' Sorry, mate. I'm not sure there's a huge market for cucumber toppers."

That phrase had his imagination going and for a split second all he saw was Kyle, face down, arse in the air, with Eric behind him with a cucumber.

Now that sounds like something I could invest in.

Deacon huffed angrily. "Those wankers don't know a good idea if they saw it. Look how many ideas they've turned down and the person goes on to make a mint." His voice grew sulky. "I thought you were my best mate."

Eric chuckled. "It's *because* I'm your best mate and Chrissy is your long-suffering wife that we are the voice of reason when you go off on one of your fad phases. Someone has to keep you from spending all my godchild's money. How long does Chrissy have to go now before I get to meet him or her?" He knew any talk of their first child would take Deke's mind off investing in silly ideas.

"She's due in four months, so still a while to go." Yep. Deacon had turned all proud papa in an instant, cucumber toppers forgotten.

Eric felt a tinge of envy and sadness. He and Linc had talked about one day having a child of their own. He swallowed the unbidden picture of his boyfriend's smiling face and spoke quickly.

"Chrissy still feeling all right though, not sick anymore? You know you need to call me if you have any concerns, right?"

"Yes, Doctor. I'm aware you'll come running down here like a mother hen should we need you."

Eric grinned. "You do know I'm not a doctor, don't you? Just a paramedic."

"There's no such thing as 'just a paramedic'," Deacon growled down the phone. "If I'm ever in some sort of accident, you can bet your balls you'd be the one I want looking out for me."

"Yeah, yeah," Eric leaned away from the wall. He needed to get on the tube. "Anyway, I'm freezing my nuts off here outside the tube station. Can I call you back later when I get home?"

"Well, you can, but if you're not interested in my cucumber idea, then I'll have to find someone else to take your place." Deacon teased. "When I make a fortune, you can bet I'll be shoving my naked arse out of the limousine mooning you as I drive by—OW! Hell, Chrissy, those are my balls you're crushing. You need those to make more babies. Don't go man- handling them like that."

Eric winced in sympathy. "I'll leave you two to your marital discord. I'll give you a buzz later, Dekes. Losing signal now. Heading into the tube station."

The air roared with all the power the world could gather, and around him, earth crumbled and split into crevasses that loomed dark and never ending. Eric cried out in fear as Lincoln went sliding toward one of the dark abysses. He scrabbled desperately for something to hold onto, finding a rock, which barely met his fingertips.

"Linc, grab my hand and hold on." Eric lay sprawled across mounds of dust and rocks, cold snow seeping into his skin, which broke and bled as shards of the injured earth sliced into him. His arm was flung out toward his boyfriend; he was trying to grab Linc's hand to stop his slow but interminable slide into dirt and deathly white. All he could see was Linc's panicked, bruised and dirty face as he tried to reach out for Eric's hand to anchor himself.

"Come on, baby, you can do it. Grab my hand." Eric slid further into the crevasse, and behind him someone tugged at his hiking boots, strong hands wrapping around his ankles, grounding him.

"I got you, Eric," shouted his colleague, Anton.

"Not going to reach," Linc panted, looking as if his arms were wrenching out of their sockets with the agonising stretch to clasp Eric's fingers. "I'm too far down to reach up and I can't stop sliding. I'm losing my grip."

"Eric," Anton's anguished voice permeated through Eric's dread. "I'm losing you. I can't hold onto you much longer." The fingers around Eric's ankles were slipping. He was gradually making his own inexorable descent into the seething mass of dust and white powder below.

"I'm not letting him go," Eric screamed against the earth's roar. "You fucking hold on to me, you tosser. Don't let me go until I've got him."

Lincoln shook his head and smiled sadly. "We're not both going." Deep blue eyes gazed into Eric's with love and regret. "Time to save yourself. I love you, baby."

Eric awoke sprawled across his bed, body slick with sweat. His heart ached from loss as fresh as if it happened yesterday. And, for a while, he was right back in Nepal trying to save the love of his life.

He punched his pillow, sobs racking his body. "Fuck. Fuck."

It had been a while since he'd had that nightmare. It had been two and a half years since he'd lost Lincoln but grief had no respect for time. It lurked deep within, ready to strike at whim.

"Fucking triggers," he muttered as he stood and walked naked over to the window of his small mid-terrace house not far from Shoreditch ambulance services. "Sometimes I hate this job."

The daily stress of attending to people in trouble, injured, or even dead, had been steadily wearing him down since he got back from Nepal.

He'd been through therapy after his return—his boss had insisted on it—but he really didn't want to go back to it now. It'd been gut wrenching enough before.

His passion for his job had deflated—losing people on the job did that to you—but he still prided himself on being the best medic he could be. The trouble was he wasn't sure that was enough when his heart wasn't in it.

Eric made himself a cup of tea in his tiny, compact kitchen and sat in the dark, sipping while scrolling through his phone. It would take some time to get back to sleep so he might as well see what was going on in the world.

He couldn't help checking out Kyle's Facebook profile. Most of his public posts were articles about making cocktails, Club Delish, snippets about music he enjoyed —IAMX being one, a group Eric enjoyed too—but there was no personal profile picture of him, only a random image of a deck of cards. In fact, there appeared to be no photos of Kyle out at dinner, with friends and none of those abominable selfies Eric hated with a passion.

Curiouser and curiouser.

Kyle seemed to be a man who preferred to keep his identity a secret. Intrigued, Eric debated whether to send a friend request. His fingers hovered over the Send button. Kyle probably wouldn't see it until tomorrow anyway, and no pain, no gain.

Request sent.

Minutes later, much to his surprise, he got a notification that Kyle had accepted. Messenger showed him as online. Eric thought it would be rude to simply leave it there, so he messaged a simple ***Hi. You're up late.***

The reply came back quickly. ***Couldn't sleep. You too?***

He smiled as he replied. ***Same. We're a right pair, aren't we?***

A smiley face came back. Not sure what to reply at four in the morning, he sent back a sleeping kitten emoji. ***Going to try get back to sleep now. Hope you do too.***

Kyle's response was a quick ***Will try. Thanks for the chat:)***

He laid his phone down and went back into his bedroom. He crawled under his duvet and lay back on his pillow, hands behind his head as he stared up at the ceiling.

"Miss you, Linc," he whispered softly into the darkness. "Gonna try to get back to sleep now. Please visit me and leave me good memories this time, will you?"

He shuffled about, punched his pillow into a comfortable nest for his head then lay down and closed his eyes.

It took him a long time to fall asleep.

Unfortunately, with a couple of his teammates calling in ill—one of them Aaron—and a horrific workload, it was impossible for Eric and Kyle to get together. Over the next couple of weeks, they texted short messages about the woe of their respective jobs and consoled themselves with silly gif wars and the occasional meme.

End of shift, he and the cleaning crew were under manpower pressure, with more needs than bodies to do the work. He figured it was a sign of things to come with the current government cutbacks and inspections. Just as he was restocking the truck, his personal mobile rang and he answered his phone with a smile. "Kyle, hey. This is a surprise—"

Out of breath, Kyle sounded panicked. "Eric, Ryan's passed out in his office. I heard this noise and came in to find him slumped over his desk. He's awake, but really out of it."

Eric's paramedic mode kicked in immediately. "Did you call nine-nine-nine? Is an ambulance on its way? I haven't heard anything via my station."

"Yes, I called them first. They're coming. They're only a few blocks away. I just wanted to tell you about it. Mango isn't here. He's abroad. I've told Ryan's bestie, Lenny, and he's going to try to track Mango down."

"Okay. Good. Chances are they'll take him to UCH. University College Hospital."

"I know what UCH stands for, Eric," Kyle said waspishly then let out a shuddering sigh. "Sorry, I'm in a state. I didn't mean to snap."

"Don't worry 'bout that. Just sort out stuff with Lenny, and let me know when they take Ryan in. Do you need to go to the hospital with him?"

Kyle heaved a deep breath. "I can't leave the club. We've got deliveries scheduled this afternoon and I'll catch shit from Ryan if I don't get it sorted. He wouldn't want the club to suffer. Lenny will go to the hospital with his boyfriend Brook. Lenny is Ryan's emergency contact anyway."

Eric didn't have time to wonder why Ryan's boyfriend wasn't down as his contact. "All right. Text me when the ambulance arrives, and I'll make a few calls to the hospital, see if I can find anything out once Ryan has been admitted. Don't worry, mate. I'm sure he's probably not been eating, or has low blood pressure or something. He's been a little off for a while now, but damned if anyone can get him to open up about it."

Kyle heaved a shuddering sigh. "Thanks. Okay. I've got to go. Lenny's on the other line. Hopefully he's got hold of Mango. Speak later."

The phone went dead and Eric swore. "Stupid, secretive arsehole, Ryan. I'm going to kick your backside when you're better."

Later that afternoon, when he had confirmation that Ryan was resting comfortably, Lenny and Brook by his side, and Mango was on his way home from Spain, Kyle texted:

Finished with deliveries. Club ready to open per usual.

Eric messaged back: ***Cool. Luckily Tuesday nights aren't that busy. Hope it goes ok.***

Kyle's reply was short. ***Yeah, me too.***

Around ten that night, Eric walked into Club Delish to find it in full swing. He grinned wryly. Life carried on regardless of the owner being in hospital.

Determined to find Kyle, Eric manoeuvred through the writhing throng of half-naked, sweaty bodies, pouting drag queens, and men in various stages of grinding and sex play on the dance floor. He had a feeling he knew where to look.

Sure enough, Kyle was in Ryan's office, standing with arms folded across his chest as he stared out of the large observation window down at the mass below. Eric couldn't help but notice the strain of Kyle's shirt across his shoulders, sleeves rolled up the elbows. His pert arse filled out his well-fitting trousers, one foot tapping to the faint strains of the music floating up from below. His hair colour had changed once again since Eric had seen him last. It was still a deep dark purple but now featured lilac streaks at the tips, and artful splashes that looked casually painted in.

Eric knocked and cleared his throat, announcing himself, knowing Kyle was skittish. Startling the man was the last thing he wanted.

"Kyle?" He waited as Kyle turned swiftly and a look of relief passed over his face when he saw it was Eric.

"Hi. What are you doing here?" Kyle moved away from the window and smiled softly. "Can't keep away, huh?"

Eric walked into the room and laid his jacket on the chair. "I wanted to see how you were doing. And find out if there was any news about Ryan. I imagine things have been a little chaotic here today."

Kyle waved a black-fingernail-tipped hand. He had long fingers, and Eric had seen their dexterity first-hand when Kyle had done his card tricks. A fleeting flash of lust passed through Eric as he wondered what those fingers would feel like milking his cock.

He realised Kyle was talking and brought himself out of his fantasy.

"Not too bad. Rufus and Greg helped offload all the deliveries and get the paperwork done while I made sure the club was ready for opening. The bar needed restocking, like badly, so I gave Jim a hand with that too."

Rufus and Greg were the club's bouncers, both fond of Ryan and Kyle. The head bartender, Jim, was a six-foot muscleman, bald and scary looking, but soft as a pussycat—until you messed with him.

Ryan had a good crew working for him.

"You heard from Lenny?" Eric wandered closer to Kyle, and now saw the dark circles under his eyes and the pallor of his face. The man looked exhausted.

Kyle nodded. "Yeah, Lenny called, said Mango had arrived. I haven't heard anything since, but he said Ryan was fine for now. He sounded worried but I didn't push him. Apparently, Ryan's gonna need some surgery but he didn't elaborate. Ryan wanted to tell me about it himself." Kyle huffed. "I don't know how that's supposed to comfort me. Now I have these horrible thoughts about cancer, or brain tumours and shit. I mean this is Ryan we're talking about." He stopped suddenly and looked uncomfortable, as if he'd said too much.

Eric hadn't missed the tremor in Kyle's voice. Quietly, he asked, "Have you eaten today? Taken a break?"

Kyle closed his eyes momentarily. "I actually can't remember. Greg offered me a doughnut at some stage but I wasn't hungry. I think he said he'd put it down here somewhere for me for later." His eyes roamed the office, looking for the pastry. Eric chuckled and walked over to the desk. He moved a wad of paperwork to reveal a Krispy Kreme doughnut box.

"It's not exactly what I'd call sustenance, but it's sweet and better than nothing." He picked up the box and handed it to Kyle. "Eat. I'll make you a black coffee. Ryan's still got that fancy coffee maker here, hasn't he?"

Kyle swiped the box, opened it and stuffed the doughnut in his mouth. "Yeah, it's in the corner over there." The words were barely distinguishable as he chewed, and he gave a deep groan that immediately had Eric thinking he'd like to be the one that made Kyle groan that way.

"Oh my God, these things are decadent but they taste so good. I could never have another thing in my mouth other than this." He burped, and gave Eric an apologetic smile as he fiddled with the coffee machine. "Sorry, and ignore that last comment. There are some other things I'd like to have in my mouth." He laughed softly.

Eric was glad to see Kyle relaxing but his comment caused desire to flood Eric's body. Those lips wrapped around his cock? Now there was a scenario he could get on board with.

Down boy, he chastised himself. You're supposed to be giving moral support, not perving over everything he says. He brought a cup of black coffee over to Kyle, who took it gratefully.

"Ta." He took a gulp and made another one of those throaty moans. Eric shifted uncomfortably and sat down on the corner of the desk, hoping the bulge in his trousers didn't show too much.

"Was that the only one?" Kyle peered over his shoulder at the desktop. "Greg didn't surprise me with another?"

There were remnants of white, powdery sugar on Kyle's lips, and Eric couldn't resist. "You have something on your lips," he murmured. He ran his thumb across the dusting and watched as Kyle's eyes darkened. He looked wary but not afraid.

"I'd like to kiss you," Eric said softly. "I don't want to scare you though. So if you say no, I'll listen. You have my word."

Kyle's breathing hitched, then with a slow smile he nodded and pulled Eric's face down to his.

Eric gave a soft gasp as their lips touched. He licked the seam of Kyle's luscious lips and his tongue came out, taunting Eric's with warm, fragrant sweetness.

Eric reached out, pulling Kyle between his legs, cupping that firm arse in his hands. Kyle moaned and his kisses became frenzied.

God, he's devouring me, sucking me in.

When they drew apart, Kyle gave a low laugh. "Wow, I didn't expect that."

Eric stared into violet eyes that were languid and glazed. "You should have. That powder on your lips begged to be kissed off."

Kyle's hands, which had been on his shoulders, moved to encircle his neck. "I think I might still have a smidgen of it left."

This time it was Kyle that took the initiative, and before long, Eric's head was swimming in a frothy swirl of desire and need. Kyle rubbed Eric's groin, and fenced him in against the wall. Eric's cock was loving where things were heading and he worried that before long he'd be left with nothing but a sticky mess in his trousers.

Pulling his mouth away from a hungry Kyle, who really seemed to *love* kissing, he managed to gasp out. "Hang on. I need a breath before I blow my load right here."

Kyle's bruised, swollen mouth pouted and his dark eyes shadowed in satisfaction. "I could really make you come just from touching and kissing you?"

"My cock certainly thinks so. Maybe we should slow down."

God, what the fuck am I saying? I've finally gone gaga. But anyone could walk in on us.

Kyle grinned wickedly. "Where's the fun in that?" He reached down and unzipped Eric's jeans as his needy dick said a happy "Hello there" when it poked up from inside his tight briefs.

Kyle licked his lips and bent down, the tip of his tongue sliding along the soft foreskin, teasing Eric to the point of insanity.

"Oh my God." He leaned back on the desk, hands splayed behind him as he watched Kyle's bobbing head. The man sucked cock like he lived for it.

The heat of his mouth, the friction and the sensation of having his cock in that warm, wet mouth drew Eric to the edge. "Kyle, better get off. I'm going to come," he gasped desperately. His legs, buttocks and back tightened at the intense feeling of his impending orgasm.

Kyle looked up, mouth glistening and wet and smiled. "Come on me," he whispered. "Want to see you spurt your spunk all over me."

Eric couldn't hold back after that filthy request. His body shuddered and he watched through glazed eyes as Kyle shrugged off his shirt, revealing a slim, tight body with toned set of abs and a treasure trail of dark hair leading down to an obviously excited thick, long cock.

That sight was all Eric needed to push him to the point of no return. He gave a loud shout and his dick let out what he thought might be a record amount of come, shooting forth in thick white streams, all over Kyle's bare stomach and chest.

Spent yet turned on beyond measure, he slumped back on the desk.

Kyle chuckled. "That's one pretty debauched sight. You flat on your back with your dick sticking out of your trousers looking like you've just been well screwed." His fingers trailed through the wetness on his chest. He dipped his forefinger in Eric's come then slowly sucked off the spunk.

Eric was mesmerised. "Hell, that mouth of yours should be classified as a WMD. In many ways."

"Clean yourself off and zip yourself up, lover boy." Kyle motioned to the bathroom. "I need to check on the club."

Eric sat up, surprised. "You don't want me to get you off? I'm more than happy to return the favour."

Kyle shrugged. "I'm good. I'll sort myself later. I don't mind a little delayed gratification." He turned, bare-chested, and wandered over to the window, where he stood again, gazing down at the strobe lit dance floor.

Eric felt a little disappointed—he'd been looking forward to seeing up-close and in-person what Kyle packed in those trousers. But he did what he was told and went into the bathroom where he tucked himself away and cleaned himself up, then stared in the mirror. His hair was mussed, his lips red and swollen, but the glow of sexual satisfaction was unmistakeable.

Kyle came in behind him and chuckled. "You do look well fucked," he said slyly. He reached over and picked up a hand towel, wetting it under the tap then cleaning the spunk off his chest and stomach. Then he sauntered out into the office. Eric followed, watching as Kyle picked up his shirt and slid it over his head. Within seconds he was the seasoned yet sexy Nightclub Manager again.

Eric picked up a stapler and toyed with it. "So, I'm back on night shift again tomorrow, but maybe we can do something during the day, if you have any time off?"

Kyle nodded absently. "Sure. Let me see how things go with Ryan. I'll message you." He turned and flashed him a smile. "I'd like to see you again."

That is a relief. I really want to see him *again. I don't want this to be a one-hit wonder.*

"Me too. This…" He flapped a hand. "This was fun. And next time, it's my turn to see you get a happy ending, *capisce*?"

"*Capisce*," Kyle acquiesced, amusement in his eyes. "I'll hold you to that."

Eric picked up his jacket and swung it over his shoulder. "Just so you know. Me coming over here tonight—it wasn't for sex or a blowjob. It was because I was worried about you."

Kyle's face softened. "I know. I appreciate it." He moved forward and enveloped Eric in a brief hug that smelt of sex and cologne. "Get home safely and text me when you do. You never know who or what's lurking out there."

"Will do. And let me know about Ryan the minute you hear anything new. I'm worried about him."

"You got it." Kyle's face split in a yawn. "God, I can't wait to get out of here tonight. Only three hours to go." He made a moue of dissatisfaction. "I think I need some more coffee to keep me awake."

Eric took Kyle's movement toward the coffee machine as his cue to leave. "See you soon. Enjoy the rest of the night." He walked out the door to the sound of coffee beans grinding.

Chapter Six

"So, you got any plans to see that hunky paramedic of yours anytime soon?"

Kyle shook his head as he leaned back in his office chair, feet planted firmly on his desk. From the other side of the desk, Lucinda grinned at him as she sucked her iced coffee through a straw. The slurping sounds had been driving him mad for a while now as he tried to finish some Club Delish social media posts and design a promotion planned for a new drag queen event later in the month.

"No, he's been busy." Kyle scowled at the paperwork in front of him. "He's a workaholic, it looks like. Anyway, with Ryan being gone, things haven't exactly been quiet here either. I don't know how he does all the stuff he does, I really don't. He must be fucking Superman."

It had been a rough time for Ryan. As Kyle had feared, things were grave; Ryan had been diagnosed with a brain tumour. After all his posturing that he'd been fine, he hadn't been fine at all. He was home now, but next week he was scheduled to have surgery to remove the bloody thing.

Kyle was scared for his friend, but at the same time angry at Ryan for waiting so long to tell anyone about it. As for Mango—well, the man had been a saint since the diagnosis and Kyle had seen a side of him he'd never expected.

Lucinda gave a loud slurp.

He glared at her. "Really? Can you finish that damn thing already?"

"Ooh, someone's in a pissy mood." She gave one last loud saucy pop as she pulled her mouth off the straw and gestured toward the desk. "Anything I can help you with before you burst a blood vessel?" She stopped as the import of her words struck her. "God, sorry. That was insensitive. Bad form, you'd say. Sorry."

He leaned back in his chair, stretching. "Don't worry. He's in good hands. The operation's scheduled for next week. Mango made him take time off so they can spend it together. I hope it all goes well. It's no picnic having a brain tumour removed."

In truth, he was petrified for Ryan. The idea of his fun-loving, dapper boss and friend having his skull opened and doctors probing around in it? Um, yuck. He shuddered.

"Have you seen him recently? How's he doing?" Lucinda stood and walked around to where he sat. She threw the offending drink container and straw in the bin and perched her bum on the desk. "And more important, sweetz, how are *you* doing? Other than stressing out at work of course. I know Ryan means a lot to you."

"I'm fine. Worried about him, of course. I saw him on Monday. He came in to check how I was coping and that his club was still functioning. He wasn't here for long though." He smiled at the memory. "Mango kept glaring at him and telling him he wasn't supposed to be here at all. Apparently, there was some DIY Ryan wanted done." He snorted with laughter. "Not Mango's forte, I don't think. He's more the 'let's pick up the deadwood and make a bridge so we can save the tigers' type of guy." Kyle batted his eyelashes modestly. "He told me I was doing a great job looking after his club. I'm glad he trusts me."

Lucinda gave an unladylike snort. "Well, duh, sweetie. You're the best at what you do." She glanced down at the trash bin. "Shit. I'm out of coffee and I can't drink that foul stuff you make. I'm gonna run down and grab another. You want one?"

Kyle nodded. "Large mocha for me. None of that pretentious shit you order. Skinny cappuccino with an extra shot, dash of vanilla, extra steaming and a great dollop of *I don't give a fuck*." He smiled wickedly. "That last bit is the free ingredient you get from the hard-done-by barista."

Lucinda tossed her hair over her shoulder with a hand. "Don't get all bitchy with me just because you haven't been boned yet by your man in uniform." Her eyes widened. "Unless you and he have…you know." She made an obscene gesture with her hand and fingers.

He flushed. "Piss off. My sex life is out of bounds to you. I still remember the last time in Vegas when you did that Photoshopped video montage of me as an Easter bunny. Rabbits running from hole to hole? That was your crazy *right* there. I'd dread to think what you'd do if I gave you any details."

She cackled. "Oh yeah. I remember that. You're lucky I only sent it to your phone. I had almost convinced the guys to put it on the big screen in the private casino for your viewing."

He laughed with her, but he was also remembering the sense of relief he'd felt when he'd deleted the vid off his phone before Mario had seen it during one of his routine mobile phone inspections. That video could have cost Kyle a broken arm or leg, or worse.

Lucinda must have sensed his mood change because she put a soft, warm hand on his cheek. "That was before I knew about your situation at home. I felt so damn bad knowing I could have got you into trouble with that douchebag."

Lucinda refused to refer to Mario as anything else. She said he'd deserved to be objectified and the term suited him better than his name. Kyle had been curious and had gone online to research the name "Mario." In various languages, it represented being male, virile, bitter, the God of War and a hammer. He'd given a humourless laugh when he'd discovered that.

"Yeah, well. He's not around anymore. Now are you going to get us that coffee or not?"

Need to change this subject. I don't want to dredge up any more bad memories.

She stuck out her tongue. "Yes, my lord. Her ladyship shall tootle off without delay." Her eyes widened. "Tootle? I never say that. It's your English vernacular rubbing off on me, mate." Her attempt at an English accent made him cringe.

Picking up her bohemian-style shawl, she wrapped it around her shoulders and made her way to the door. "I'll pick us a couple of doughnuts too. Sprinkles for you?"

He nodded, his groin warming at the thought of what had happened the last time he'd eaten a doughnut. "Sounds good. Now bugger off and leave me in peace for a minute. I have something to finish."

He watched fondly as she flounced out the door. He didn't know where he'd be without her. It was a pity her home was across the pond.

His mobile buzzed. He grinned when he saw the caller ID. Eric. "Hi there. How are things going?"

"They're good. Been working my arse off but got a few days off now." Eric sounded tired. "I have some family commitments. My sister's getting married tomorrow. She's in Somerset with my folks, so I'll be driving there in the morning. I have tonight free though, and I was chancing that we might be able to get together for a drink or something?"

Kyle's stomach gave a strange flutter. "I love the offer, but it's Friday night and the club will be packed. And with Ryan not being here…" His voice trailed off. "Sorry, but I doubt I'll escape long enough to take a pee, let alone have a drink."

Eric's sigh echoed down the phone. "I thought as much. This isn't going to be easy, is it?"

Kyle was confused. "What isn't going to be easy?"

"Getting to see you again." The smile in Eric's voice made those butterflies in Kyle's stomach speed up. "Our working lives are definitely not conducive to courting someone."

He swallowed. "Courting someone?"

He almost felt Eric's shrug. "Well, yeah," he replied. "Trying to at least." He laughed softly and Kyle's insides turned to mush.

God, that man sounds sexy. His laugh is like honey poured over a Belgian waffle. Sweet and decadent.

"I have the usual time off, Sunday and Monday. When do you get back from your family wedding?"

"I plan on leaving Sunday morning. My mum won't let me leave without feeding me a full English before I go. Dad will probably want to shoot the breeze about the latest developments in apple farming."

"Your folks have a farm?" Kyle was enchanted. He'd always lived in cities, even as a kid, and often yearned for a bit of outdoor space and greenery, complete with the requisite baby pig, lamb and, possibly, even a dog.

Eric chuckled. "Yeah, my dad grows apples and makes cider for some of the local markets. It's not a huge place, but it was a great place to grow up in." His tone grew fond. "Shelley—my sister who's getting married tomorrow—and I used to be run around the orchards, helping my dad pick the fruit. We'd eat a lot of it, and give ourselves tummy aches. Good times."

"Sounds great," Kyle said wistfully. "I've never been on a farm before."

"Never?" Eric said in surprise. "We can't have that. I'll have to take you down to see it one day. Meet the folks."

There was a long pause then Eric spoke again, sounding a little uncomfortable. "I mean, you know, as a friend. Not like to introduce you to the parents and declare undying love. Crap, I'm really digging myself a hole here, aren't I?"

Kyle laughed. "I get it. Don't worry. I'm not expecting a ring or anything. Visiting your farm would be cool."

"Good." Eric's relief was palpable. "Anyway, back to the whole date thing. I'm pretty sure I can wangle Monday off somehow. I have a colleague who owes me a favour. Perhaps we can meet for dinner somewhere, maybe that restaurant called Galileo's in Soho? Ryan says it's well worth a visit. Apparently, a lot of people he knows eat there and rave about it."

Kyle was interrupted from replying as Lucinda walked in. She held up his coffee and he nodded his thanks. She sat down in her spot and the slurping noises commenced. He shook his head at her in irritation. Her answer was to slurp louder.

Glaring at his friend, he realised he hadn't replied yet. "Yes, that sounds great. Are you sure it's open? A lot of restaurants close on Mondays."

"It's open," Eric assured him. "They're open all week round, I think. Shall we say seven-thirty?"

"Suits me fine," Kyle confirmed.

"Okay, see you Monday. I look forward to it." Eric rang off.

"You have a date then?" Lucinda asked around a mouthful of what looked like chocolate chip cookie. She nudged the white box over to him, indicating his doughnut inside. He sighed as he picked it up. "Yes. Sort of. Dinner at Galileo's."

Lucinda's eyes lit up. "Ooh, I've heard about that place. Didn't it just win a Glass Clove Award for the most promising venue of the year?"

"I have no idea. I don't read the gossip and social magazines like you do." He bit into his doughnut and gave a blissful moan. "God, this tastes good. Although it's going straight to my damn hips."

His friend stuck her middle finger up. "What damned hips? You're all lean and muscled. It's *my* hips you should be worrying about. I might have to buy two seats to fly back to the U.S. at the rate I'm eating these things." She gestured to her cookie. "I think I might be addicted to these peanut butter choc chip ones."

Kyle knew the feeling. If he didn't watch out, he may be in danger of getting addicted to the sexy stud muffin called Eric Kirby.

Saturday night at the club, Kyle was run off his feet. He'd been persuasive enough to coerce Lucinda into helping him. She'd assisted Jim getting the bar organised, and checked out the restrooms. She had refused to step foot in the hedonistic bathroom known as Deep Purple— Kyle had to face that one himself. Now, from the looks of it, she was entertaining the patrons. She was up on stage with Molly Luscious, one of the regular drag queen acts. Lucinda was dressed up as Charlie Chaplin, hat and cane at the ready, and she and Molly were no doubt trading insults and bitchiness.

He turned to fish out Ryan's secret whisky stash in his bottom desk drawer, opened it up and poured a shot, which Kyle tossed back like a boss.

Wow, that tastes surprisingly good. So smooth.

He took another swig then set the glass down on the desk.

Another two hours to go and he'd be on his way home. Lucinda was staying with him tonight as she planned on having brunch nearby with some friends in the morning. He'd be glad of her company. And he still had his dinner date with Eric to look forward to.

Kyle smiled dreamily. Eric was something else. He was warm and funny, and when he was around, Kyle felt safe. Cherished. It had been a long time since anyone had made him feel that way.

Still daydreaming about the man in his life, he turned and walked over to his office door, intending to walk down and check on how things were going with Rufus and Greg. As he opened the door, he was met with a wall of grey button-down shirt and black jeans. The man reeked of expensive bourbon. He stood there, hand held up as if to knock on his door. His face was flushed, looking truly pissed off. Kyle could feel the waves of anger coming off him.

A frisson of fear crept down his spine, and for a moment he was frozen on the spot. He cleared his throat, hand on the doorknob, ready to smash it closed should this guy be a threat of any kind.

"Can I help you?" Kyle enquired, trying to keep his voice even.

The stairs to the office were marked as "Private/No entry" but there was nothing stopping anyone coming up to see him. It happened all the time.

"I dunno, mate. Can you? Where is she?" the man slurred, taking a step forward. Kyle instinctively stepped back.

"Where is who?"

Man Mountain stepped forward. "My girlfriend, you tosser. She went out to use the bathroom and I haven't seen 'er since. Someone said she came up here."

"She's not here, mate. I haven't seen any ladies up here." He held up a hand, and pointed behind him. "Why don't we go downstairs, see if we can find her? Perhaps she's got lost or stepped out for a smoke."

"Nancy doesn't smoke, you twat." The man's eyes were red, his mouth a snarl, and Kyle tried to stave off the panic rising in his chest.

"Then perhaps she's in the bathroom." He swallowed as the man took another step toward him. There wasn't much saliva in his dry mouth.

Please God, don't let me find her lost in Deep Purple. I don't think Ryan could afford the trauma payments when she sues the club.

"I knew this was a mistake coming here. Gay clubs aren't for ladies like my Nance," the man spat. "Guys can tell a bird they're gay but be straight and get them to do all sorts, like show their tits off. I've seen it." He glared balefully at Kyle. "Have you seen 'em then? Nance's tits?"

"Sir, I can assure you no one has been up here and I most certainly haven't seen anyone's tits." He was finding it hard to breathe as the man pressed closer. The familiar tingle of fear spread from his insides to his extremities. "And I can assure you I have no desire to do so. I'm a real gay, not a pseudo one. Now can we go downstairs to try and find her?"

The man raised his fist menacingly and pushed Kyle back with his other meaty hand. "Not before I check this room, make sure she's not 'ere. Move over."

Kyle stood to one side as Man Mountain brushed roughly past him. He took a few deep breaths and willed his heart to slow down.

This isn't Mario. This is nothing like Mario. One, two, three....

He hoped someone had seen the man come upstairs and had followed to investigate. He wasn't the right size to fight a guy like this, and it wasn't as if he had any ninja skills or anything.

"Nancy, darlin', are you here? Come out, sweetie. I won't be angry, I promise," Man Mountain cooed as he searched the office. It didn't take long. The office wasn't big and apart from the small en-suite bathroom, there were no doors other than the one leading to the stairs.

Man Mountain's face grew darker as his search turned up nothing. He pivoted swiftly and punched the wall next to Kyle. His head swam as he ducked down, instinctively raising his arms in front of his face. His gut churned and he wanted to vomit. Plaster exploded in fragments, covering him with fine dust and shards.

Not the dark touch, please. Not again.

Kyle's vision swam and for one sickening moment Mario's voice echoed in his head.

You asked for it, you slut. It's your fault I'm like this. You've infected me with your body and those cow eyes. Bend over and get ready for a beating. God lets me punish sinners like you.

"I wasn't going to hit you, mate. No need to look so scared." Man Mountain's voice toned softened. When Kyle looked up he could see the guy was puzzled, as if he couldn't believe his behaviour could cause such a reaction.

Kyle wasn't taking chances. He scrabbled up, moving toward the door, and in his haste, his backside hit the desk, the corner sinking deep into the back of his buttock. The pain radiated down his leg and he gasped. "Shit, that hurts."

The guy's expression turned to concern and he shuffled towards him. "You okay, mate?"

Kyle managed to speak. Just. His buttock throbbed and he was coated with fear. "Yes. Go. Away. Your girlfriend isn't here. You can see that." He motioned desperately around him, hating that he felt so helpless. Useless. "Go downstairs and look for her. I'm sure if you look hard enough you'll find her."

Maybe she ran away from your sorry, bullying arse. I wouldn't blame her. That's what I did.

The guy looked confused for a second then his face cleared. "Yeah, she isn't here, is she? Whoever said she'd come up here must have been mistaken."

Give the gorilla a banana, Kyle thought viciously. Hell, give him a fucking bunch.

"No, she isn't. Now piss off."

The guy ambled to the door, looking shamefaced. "Sorry, mate," he said apologetically. "I wasn't goin' to hurt ya. Sometimes my temper gets the better of me."

You don't say.

Now that Kyle was feeling a little safer, his catty side couldn't resist a parting shot. "I'm sure you two deserve each other."

The guy nodded, a dreamy grin on his face. "We're getting married in September. She's gonna be Mrs. Lloyd Glasscock then." He smiled proudly.

Despite his recent panic, Kyle smothered a giggle of hysteria. He thought perhaps he might have to send a sympathy card to the unfortunate Nancy having a surname like that. Poor kids if ever there were any.

"I'm sure you'll be very happy together," he managed between gritted teeth.

Lloyd nodded and left the office.

No sooner had he gone than Kyle closed and locked the door. He strode over to the desk and poured a stiff whisky then knocked it back. He knew that lately he was drinking more than he should, but by God, he needed this right now.

He was starting to feel a little buzzed. Between nearly getting beaten up, not eating anything substantial, and imbibing two hefty glasses of Ryan's treasured ten-year-old Ardbeg, Kyle wasn't surprised he felt his knees wobble.

His hands shook as he poured himself another, and then he closed his eyes, feeling the burn of the whisky as it traced a path down his throat. Perhaps it would wash away the taste of shame and self-loathing at the fact he'd fallen to pieces.

Again.

Light burnt his eyelids and seared into his brain. Kyle opened one bleary eye and looked around. He didn't recognise the place he was lying in, so he closed his eyes again. There was a chuckle from somewhere above him, and once again he opened his eyes and stared about blearily. He vaguely made out the figure of Lucinda sitting curled up in the bench window overlooking the street below.

He was still at the club.

He groaned loudly and sat up. His head throbbed liked two ninjas were battling it out with nunchaku and flying stars. "Oh shit," he croaked. "What did I do?"

"You drank nearly half a bottle of Ryan's treasured whisky, passed out on the desk and spent the night here. As did I." Lucinda uncurled her long limbs and strode over to where he lay. He now recognised the couch in the office as being his resting place.

"Jim and I managed to get your sorry arse onto the couch, and then after we locked up, he made up one of the private cubicles downstairs into a sleeping pad with blankets, and that's where I slept."

"I'm sorry. I didn't mean to pass out. I was just…" his voice tailed off.

Lucinda smirked. "Having a party for one, it looked like. Did you even eat yesterday?"

Kyle shook his head and wished he hadn't. "I don't think so. Fuck, my head hurts."

Lucinda handed him a couple of tablets and a glass of water. "I thought you might need these. It's Advil. Get it down you." She frowned. "What got into you anyway? It's not usual for you to overindulge like that."

He didn't want to tell her the truth—that a man had frightened him, made him think of his past, his inadequacies, his shame. He'd told her he was dealing with it, but there were those loitering pockets of angst and uncertainty when he found himself in situations he thought he couldn't control; then it all came rushing back.

Kyle swallowed the pills with water then lay back on the couch and closed his eyes. "Everything caught up with me, I guess. Worried about Ryan. I just needed to blow off some steam."

She regarded him and for a split second it was as if she knew he was lying. Then she shrugged. "We all have those times. But if anything is wrong, I expect you'd tell me about it, yeah? That's why we're besties."

"Thanks, Luce. I know you're always there for me." He grinned wryly. "Like now. It can't have been comfortable sleeping downstairs and I'm so sorry I made you do that. You could have taken a taxi back to your hotel and left me sleeping it off."

She pulled a moue. "Nah, where's the fun in that? Someone has to look after you." She gestured at the half-full bottle on the desk. "Although you'll need to replace that before Ryan gets back. That'll cost you about fifty dollars."

Kyle sniffed. "I know a man who'll get it for me for much less."

Lucinda frowned. "Unless it was his special bottle of whisky that was bottled in about the nineteen-sixties. Jim said he had one of those somewhere. In which case, it'll cost close to three and a half thousand dollars. Can your friend get you one of *those* cheap?"

Kyle's stomach rebelled and he felt the beginning of a retch. He desperately sought out the dustbin. Lucinda sighed and pushed it over with her foot. Bile left his stomach and splattered at the bottom of the wads of paper that lay there. He wiped his mouth and prayed to every god he knew.

"Please tell me it wasn't that one?" he gasped. "I just picked the bottle from the top tier. Surely he wouldn't keep something worth that much here in his office?"

Lucinda pursed her lips, eyes alight with devilment. "Let me see…" She picked up the bottle and tut-tutted.

He waited, mind racing.

I'll have to empty my savings to buy that. Shit, why didn't I take more notice of what the fuck I was drinking?

He hadn't realised he wasn't breathing until she spoke.

"You're in luck. It's the bog standard one." Her grin flashed and she put the bottle down. Kyle let out a sigh of relief. "But I knew that. God, you are so gullible."

"You bitch," Kyle sputtered. "Why would you do that to me?"

"I had to sleep in a smelly club on a sofa where guys banged each other all night. I'm probably covered in all sorts of disgusting stuff. You deserved it."

His eyes narrowed. "You stepped over a line, there, Missy. I will get you back for that one. You made me hurl."

She stood up and came over to flick his nose. "Nuh-huh. That was all on you, pretty boy. You and that bottle of whisky." Her voice softened, but there was an edge to it he recognised. "God knows what made you drink so much. Are you sure there's nothing you want to tell me?"

He crossed his fingers. In the past, he'd never been able to keep secrets from her. She'd read him like a book. It was just as well, or he'd most likely be dead right now at the hands of his ex-lover. "Give it up, Sherlock. Can't a man get drunk, pass out and have his lady friend take care of him?"

Lucinda's face shadowed. "Yeah, it's just that..."

Kyle knew what she was thinking. *It's just that every time you did that in the past was after Mario had hurt you, and you chose solace in booze and hid away like a cornered animal.*

Kyle had never worried that his self-despair would turn into alcoholism. The one and only thing he'd had control over back then was his drinking, and he'd been damned if Mario would take that away from him as well.

He struggled to his feet, giving a startled yelp as his head buzzed with dizziness. "Honest, I'm good." He sniffed himself and grimaced. "I need to shower though. We'd best get to my place. Unless you want to go back to your hotel?"

Lucinda slid off the edge of the desk. "I'll come home with you, make sure you get there all right. Then I'll probably get a taxi back to the hotel and have a shower myself. I stink of spunk."

She stuck out her tongue and he couldn't help a tired laugh. She was amazing and he missed her so much when she wasn't around.

"Fine. Let me hide the evidence of my self-indulgence and we'll get a taxi. I know it's not far but I don't think I want to walk home looking like this."

Chapter Seven

Eric tapped his fingers on the bar top, picked at the beer bottle's label, then drew a long pull as he glanced towards the restaurant's entrance. Seven-thirty. Kyle should be here any minute.

The butterflies in his stomach intensified as the minutes ticked passed. There was something about Kyle that brought out all Eric's protective instincts. He couldn't shake the feeling that someone, an ex perhaps, hadn't treated Kyle well. He was edgy, skittish and…oh my God, the man was gorgeous.

Eric took a deep breath as Kyle walked in the door. His fluid motion was a thing of beauty as his amazing long legs carried him into the restaurant. When he spotted Eric at the bar, Kyle's face burst into a wide smile, and Eric imagined he was the only person in the room enjoying its warmth and radiance.

God, I'm really into this guy.

Kyle's shock of purple black hair was covered with a grey beanie, giving his face an elfin appearance. His dark burgundy jeans were offset with a tight V-neck white tee-shirt, and covered with a casual black jacket teamed with a funky brown and red patterned scarf. He looked stunningly casual and elegant at the same time.

Eric looked down at his brown chinos with his black button up shirt and felt a little dowdy. But when Kyle's eyes lit up at the sight of him and roved down Eric's body, hovering in a frank, groin-warming inspection, he felt marginally better.

"You look edible," Kyle murmured. "You are red-haired all over, it would seem." He reached out and caressed the chest curls poking out of Eric's shirt. "Of course, I speak from experience." One eyebrow lifted teasingly, the one with the barbell piercing.

Eric felt his face flame at the reminder of that hot, dirty blowjob at the club. He'd be lying if he said he hadn't thought that getting another was on his To Do list tonight, first date or not. "Um, yeah, same colour all over." Eric laughed as the waitress behind the bar gave him a knowing look. "You look really good too. That beanie suits you."

Kyle chuckled. He reached up and tugged it off, running fingers through his hair to tame it. "It itches," he complained. "But it keeps my ears warm. I feel the cold sink into me from head to toe."

Eric touched Kyle's arm. "Do you want a drink at the bar, or do you want to go straight to the table?"

Kyle's eyes gleamed. "Table sounds good," he murmured. "A little more private than here."

Eric cleared his dry throat. "Sure." He gestured to the waitress who was smiling like a Cheshire cat. "Could we be taken to our table please?"

Settled at a small table for two in the back corner, drinks in hand, Kyle looked around in interest. "It's the first time I've been here." He scanned the room as he drank his white wine. "It looks incredible with this décor, and the ambience is great. Really puts you at ease."

Eric nodded. "Yeah, I've been in restaurants where you feel a bit out of place, and can't relax. This one is different. Makes you feel welcome."

"Someone Ryan knows owns it. A guy called Gideon Kent. Apparently, he gave up cooking for a while because of an accident, but now he's back, and his boyfriend is the head chef. Nothing like keeping it in the family." Kyle watched Eric over the rim of his glass then asked, "How did your sister's wedding go?"

The change of subject caught Eric off guard. "It was"—he hesitated—"a wedding. The usual palaver accompanied by a wedding dress, pomp and ceremony plus too much food and drink. My folks did Shelley well. Her husband Greg is a really great guy." Eric grinned. "Luckily, she's the only daughter, so they don't have to splash out on anything for me or my younger brother, Shepherd. I'm not big on the whole being married thing and Shepherd..." He snorted. "That kid is never going to settle down. He's in Thailand now writing his travel journal to add to the video for his YouTube channel. Next week he's in Bangkok and God knows where he'll go from there. He has a girl in every port and loves it." Part of him envied Shep's lifestyle. At twenty-four years old, the world was his oyster.

Kyle's eyebrows rose. "Shepherd is a YouTuber? Wow. It amazes me how people make money out of that. So, you're not into marriage?"

Eric shrugged. "Marriage is just a piece of paper. It's the relationship and how you live your life together that matters. Don't get me wrong, I cheered like a football fan when gay marriage was legalised in the U.K., but it's not important to me personally."

Despite his parents being together for over thirty years, Eric wasn't a believer in the whole formal commitment thing. He and Lincoln had differing views on the matter, which led to a few loud arguments over the years. But now, every so often, Eric wondered if he had been stupid not to accede to Linc's wishes. Hindsight and regret in the rear-view mirror.

Kyle took a sip of his wine, probably contemplating what Eric had said. The waiter came over and they ordered their food.

Eric couldn't help but notice Kyle's nails were clear tonight, no colourful varnish. They were well-maintained, oval-shaped and slightly longer than Eric had seen on a man before. He liked it. Those nails raking down his back…he shuddered. *Down boy*. Stop being so damned shallow. Not everything is about sex.

Although…a lot of the time it was.

"So," Kyle drawled. "We have something else in common. Neither of us are big believers in the whole matrimonial thing." His face darkened. "And having to get married in church or utter those awful wedding vows—that really doesn't work for me."

Eric nodded. "I remember you told Ryan and I once you aren't religious. I'm not either so looks like we have that in common too." He frowned. "You said we have something else in common. What was the other thing?"

Kyle's eyes lit up and his mouth quirked up a little. "We both love dick," he announced, not as quietly as Eric would have liked. Then Kyle sat back and laughed as Eric glanced around quickly to see if anyone had heard.

"Why not proclaim it to the whole restaurant?" Eric murmured, but smiled at his dinner partner. *God, the man was adorable.*

Kyle's fingers grazed Eric's, sending a shock down his arm. "Why shouldn't we? We're two grown gay men on a date. I won't hide who I am." He looked uncertain suddenly, and sat back, biting his lip. It was a most endearing gesture. "You're not, like, in the closet or anything, are you? I mean, I don't expect naked shagging in public, but I won't hide the fact I'm with a man." His voice grew fierce. "That's pretty much a deal breaker for me."

Eric was taken aback. "No. Hell, I'm out and fine with it. I mean, I try to watch what I do in public but it's not like I wouldn't hug or kiss, or hold hands with a guy, as long it's safe."

Kyle leaned forward and traced the blue vein in Eric's hand. "Good. Because I've done that before for someone and I can't do it again."

Eric hadn't missed the pain in Kyle's tone, and once again he wondered who had hurt him. Now wasn't the right time to ask about it.

"So, I've told you about my family. Tell me about yours." Eric waved the waiter over to order more drinks. "I know you're Jewish, non-religious and worked in Vegas as a croupier or something like that, but not much else."

Eric watched the shutters come down over Kyle's face. It reminded him of a veil being drawn over a bride.

"Not much to tell, really. I was born in Chicago. My parents emigrated to the U.K. when I was seven." His fingers toyed nervously with the saltshaker. "I went back to Las Vegas in oh-eight, when I was twenty, waited to turn twenty-one then found work as a croupier-slash-cocktail waiter at The Bohemian Club Casino. That's where I met Lucinda." His face lit up and Eric hoped that one day he might see the same affection on Kyle's face for him. "She's my bestie, although we live on different continents. I'd love you to meet her while she's here."

He put the saltshaker down. "Then in oh-eleven I moved back to the UK and bummed around a bit. A year later I joined Club Delish. I've been there ever since."

Eric nodded. "No family then?"

Kyle looked down at the table. His movements stilled. "I'm an only child. Mum and Dad moved back to Chicago seven years ago. I see them when I go back to the States." His brow furrowed. "That would have been June last year."

"You liked Las Vegas then? It must have been exciting, being out there with all that glam and high rollers."

Kyle's hands clenched on the table, scrunching his napkin into a tight wad. "It was an experience. Let's simply say that." He looked relieved as the food arrived. "This looks scrumptious. Smells amazing."

Eric had a feeling the sharing portion of the evening had concluded. He guessed both of them had their secrets. You couldn't get through your twenties without amassing some baggage. Eric had his Lincoln stuff, and Kyle…well he had something, that was for sure.

Eric was happy to wait until things were at a place that they both felt comfortable to say more. He had high hopes things would progress in that direction.

They ate in companionable silence, joking and putting the world to rights. Eric was all for paramedics being given bulletproof vests and being taught how to deal with potential bombs and explosive devices. Kyle was keen to ensure the future of nightclubs in London, given new legislation, increasing bureaucracy and the focus on shutting down clubs to make way for offices. Money talked in a loud voice in the new London.

Their conversation took them late into the night, and it was close to eleven when they both sat back, replete with coffee, and stared at each other.

Kyle cleared his throat. "I guess we should be getting on our way. The staff keeps giving us the evil eye. I think they want to close." He laughed softly. "I know the feeling, so what do you say we take the chit-chat back to my place, have a nightcap and see what develops."

Eric blinked. He'd never met anyone quite as direct as Kyle before.

"Unless you have an early morning shift tomorrow," Kyle hastened to add. "It's Monday, so I'm off. I guess you don't have the same privilege." He looked hopeful.

"My shift starts at ten," Eric said quietly.

"Oh." Kyle seemed uncomfortable. "Look, I'm sorry if I'm moving too fast for you, it's just…I like you and I'm not one to beat around the bush. I understand if you'd rather let this one go. Just tell me."

Eric laughed softly. He loved the way Kyle tackled everything head on, and wore his heart (or was it his cock?) on his sleeve. After a few tough years of being unable to care about anyone after Linc, this colourful man was a refreshing change, and Eric couldn't wait to get to know him better.

Kyle cocked his head. "Was that a 'I can't wait to kick him to the kerb' laugh or a 'I'm going to take him up on his offer and soon we'll be naked' one?"

Eric stood. "It's an 'I'm going to take a piss and while I'm gone you get the bill so we can go home together' laugh." He watched a grin slide onto Kyle's handsome face then turned to walk to the bathroom. *This guy is going to be a whole load of trouble. But I think I'm ready for it. God, please don't let me have any nightmares tonight.*

Eric hadn't had any bad dreams in the last week so he was hopeful. The thought of going home with Kyle both exhilarated and scared him. Eric did his business, zipped up and by the time he got back, Kyle was already standing with his jacket slung over his shoulder.

"I thought you were getting the bill?"

"I did. Done and dusted." Kyle grinned.

"The idea wasn't that you were paying. How much do I owe you?" Eric reached into his pocket for his wallet. His hand brushed the cock that had been half-hard all night.

Kyle tut-tutted. "Simmer down, gorgeous. You can pay me back later, or get the next one. I thought we could do with getting a move on, that's all." His violet eyes flashed, heat visible in their depths.

Even empty, the restaurant seemed small and crowded suddenly and Eric hoped Kyle didn't live too far. "Let's go then." Eric noticed the huskiness in his voice, and from Kyle's full body shiver, he'd noticed too. "I'm in the mood for a nightcap."

The taxi ride was so brief that as soon as they were settled inside, they were pulling up to the block of flats where Kyle lived. The building's façade was old and Victorian.

Eric insisted on paying the taxi driver then followed Kyle inside.

"It's only four levels," Kyle explained as they walked up the winding stairs. "Three flats on each floor. Mine is at the end of the fourth floor." He flashed a wicked grin. "The lift kinda groans when you get in it, so I prefer the stairs most times."

Eric loved walking behind Kyle. He was almost at full mast already just from watching the globes of the man's arse as they worked together in tandem temptation.

What this man does to me is criminal.

They stopped in front of a scratched, white oak door and Kyle slid the key in and opened it. He stepped inside, flipped on the light switch then shrugged off his scarf and jacket, and threw his beanie casually on a chair.

"Make yourself at home." He gestured to the couch. "I'll grab us a drink. You like whisky?"

Eric nodded as he sat down. "That's fine, thanks."

God, he wanted to make a move on Kyle. To grab him, pull him over Eric's body and kiss the ever-loving fuck out of him. To strip him, see what delights he held hidden beneath those trendy clothes, and to be lust-driven, sweaty beasts together, intent on finding their gratification. The need was so strong Eric could taste it in the air, scent it in the tantalising aroma of spicy cologne and musky male.

Kyle coughed. "Your drink, sir?" He passed the glass to Eric and sat down beside him, close enough that he felt the heat emanating from Kyle's body. The smirk on his face said he knew exactly what he wanted. Eric imagined he mirrored Kyle's open desire.

As Eric's first sip of whisky slid into that mouth, Kyle's gaze was riveted to Eric's throat. Those intriguing violet eyes flared as Eric swallowed and Kyle took a sip of his own drink. His tongue came out and licked the remnants of whisky from his lips. Surely intentional, the tease hit its mark, raising Eric's blood pressure and making his groin ache.

"Maybe the drink can wait." Kyle's raspy voice drifted to Eric's ears like warm air. Kyle—whose hands shook ever so slightly—took Eric's drink from him.

Eric waited, happy to let Kyle take the lead. Kyle leaned over and ran his pink, wet tongue down the length of Eric's throat. Kyle's lips lingered on the throbbing pulse, matching the sensation in Eric's trousers of his hard-on pressing against his chinos.

"You taste so good," Kyle whispered as he licked blissful strokes down Eric's skin. "You should have your own flavour ice cream."

Eric laughed softly as his hands encircled the other man's waist and pulled him closer. Kyle went one better, twisting and straddling Eric's lap, tantalisingly brushing his groin with a tight, round arse.

"I'm not sure about that," Eric murmured, holding Kyle's gaze as Eric unzipped Kyle's jeans, releasing him. Eric swiped his fingers over the tip, loving the velvet-wet smoothness. "I bet you taste just as good."

Kyle's pupils expanded, and his breathing quickened.

The kiss that followed was everything Eric could have hoped for. Kyle's mouth was nubile, eager, and the way he pressed his body against Eric's with each frantic thrust of tongue drove Eric crazy. He didn't even hear or feel his own trousers being unzipped, though he saw Kyle rising above him with a desperation borne of need.

"I need skin, friction," Kyle panted as he pushed his own smooth hardness against Eric's. A warm hand reached down and slicked him up with his own wetness. "I've been waiting all night to do this."

Eric mumbled, "I'm not resisting," between greedy kisses and groping hands that seemed to be everywhere at once. "This is me agreeing with you."

Kyle chuckled, a strangled sound as he ground his shaven groin harder against Eric's. Eric laid his head back on the couch, a moan of pleasure escaping from his ravaged mouth. "We're gonna have friction burns on our dicks." Even as he said it, he slid his hands into the back of Kyle's jeans and roughly held him tighter. The globes of that tight arse felt magical in Eric's hands and he could think of a lot of other things he'd like to do with them.

Kyle's reply was to rub harder and Eric zoned out, closing his eyes as delectable sensations raced through his body.

Time and space disappeared to become only having this sexy man on top of him, taking his mouth with a savage intensity that made Eric see stars. Kyle's soft moans, the tickling of skin as his hair brushed Eric's skin—they all came together in one soul-shattering realisation that Eric had missed this.

Missed having someone so focused on him, giving him pleasure.

It had been too long, and Eric wanted more of it.

"Oh, God," Kyle whispered as he strained above. "I hope you don't mind a mess…" The last words were lost in a deep groan as Kyle came, warm fluid soaking Eric's groin and stomach. Spurts of spunk hit the underside of Eric's chin, catapulting him over the edge. He clasped the bum beneath his hands tighter, fingers clenching as he released.

Again, swollen lips smashed against his. Eric needed to draw breath, so after what seemed like minutes, he pulled away.

There was a moment of blissful silence. Both men lay stuck together by come and sweat.

Kyle chuckled. "Nice. I think we might have invented a new form of liquid Velcro. I don't think I can move away."

Eric grinned, his body coming down from his orgasmic high. "We'd have a lot of gay men volunteering to create the product if it came to that."

The absurdity of that image made them both giggle like kids. It had been a long time since Eric had heard that sound emanating from his own throat.

"We need to clean up," he murmured into Kyle's cute shell of an ear. "Before we stay this way forever."

"Is that such a bad thing?" Kyle murmured back. "I'm pretty comfy here." He nuzzled Eric's neck and planted a soft kiss there. "You make me feel good about myself. Like I'm worth something."

A surge of affection swept through Eric. Kyle was a playful kitten—one with claws, judging from how his sharp fingernails had dug into Eric's arms. Kyle was warm, fragrant and seemed to love cuddling, something Eric was partial to.

He kissed the top of Kyle's fragranced hair. "Whoever it was that made you feel you weren't worth anything was a damned idiot. They had no idea what they had. I guess I'm the lucky one now." He didn't miss Kyle's hitch of breath and the way his hands grasped tighter around Eric's waist.

His playful kitten obviously had some issues. Eric wondered what had happened to make him that way.

Eric cleared his throat. "You're heavy, and I need to piss. I think you're sitting on my bladder."

Kyle grumbled as he lifted himself off. "Fine, spoilsport. Way to ruin the mood with talk of your bodily needs, other than the ones we just satisfied."

Eric couldn't help laughing. "It's either that or I do it here, and as much as I'd like to stay here with you, the idea of wetting myself isn't one I want to entertain." He stood but didn't bother zipping himself up.

"Yeah? You like being with me then?" The vulnerability in Kyle's tone made Eric turn around. Kyle stared up, a picture of debauched beauty lying on the couch. His pale face held a slight frown and he was biting the skin at the side of his nail.

"I think I just proved that, didn't I?"

Kyle pushed himself up on his elbows, an adorable scowl starting on his face.

Eric hastened to qualify his words. "I mean, I'm not here just for the sex, okay? I like you. I like your company." His bladder protested at being delayed but he didn't want to leave while Kyle still thought he was nothing more than a warm body to get off with.

Kyle snorted. "Okay then. Glad we got that sorted. You're sleeping over, right?"

Eric nodded.

Kyle's face softened. "You're jiggling. Go to the bog, for God's sake." He stood and motioned to the door leading off the lounge. "I'll get cleaned up after you. The bedroom is through there."

Eric nodded and sped off to the bathroom to both empty his bursting bladder and clean up. He managed as best he could, taking his briefs and chinos off to wipe off some of the mess. He grimaced. Even so, he'd have to wear them crusty in the morning on his walk of shame. He took a deep breath and wandered out and across to the bedroom.

Kyle was sitting on the side of the bed. He raised an eyebrow when he saw Eric's attire.

"I like the no-pants look." He got up and gestured to the left side of the bed. "Mine's the right side. Get comfortable. I'll be back in a moment." He gestured to the dresser in the corner. "If you fancy sleeping in anything, there's stuff in the top drawer."

Eric took off his shirt and slid naked into the bed. He'd never been able to sleep with clothes on; he hoped Kyle wouldn't mind.

He caught his breath when Kyle walked back into the room. Lithe, with muscles in all the right places and long legs with a smattering of fine hair, he reminded Eric of a thoroughbred colt.

Kyle slipped in beside him. "Mmm, nice," he purred. "I like a man with nothing on lying next to me." He leaned back against the pillows and regarded Eric with a smouldering stare.

"Oh no, mate, no more tonight." Eric got comfortable and snuggled down into the duvet. "As tempting as you are, I need some sleep. If we start again now, it'll be hours before I finish with you and you'll be screaming for more."

"Ooh," Kyle muttered. "You're a confident one. What makes you think I won't be the one making *you s*cream?" He smirked. "Next time, we fuck. Properly."

Eric's cock stirred and he ignored it and closed his eyes. "Uh-huh," he managed sleepily. "Maybe next time we can have an all-night fuck fest but tonight, I need some zzzzs. Work tomorrow. Remember? Not like some of us who have Monday off."

He sensed Kyle's face near and his warm breath on Eric's cheeks. He opened his eyes and noticed for the first time Kyle's real eyes were a deep, dark brown. As much as Eric loved the violet contacts, the hue of that brown made him think of warm chestnuts and cold winter days.

"I like the sound of next time," Kyle murmured as his lips found Eric's in a lingering kiss. "I'll hold you to it. 'Night."

Kyle pressed his front against Eric's back. "You don't mind me being the big spoon, do you?" he whispered drowsily. "I promise to keep my bits in control."

"'S fine," Eric mumbled. "Go to sleep, Kyle."

There was another soft drift of lips against the back of Eric's neck and then he remembered no more.

Chapter Eight

"Hey, big guy. What are you smiling about? Looks like you got some last night."

Eric turned to see Aaron watching him. He finished packing in some of the stock he needed for their shift and grinned back.

"Maybe I did, maybe I didn't." He closed the back of the truck and went over to give his partner a shoulder slap. "How are you doing on that front? Did you go on that date your bubbie set up for you?"

Aaron's face brightened. "Actually, I did. It went pretty well. She's a nice girl."

Eric raised an eyebrow. "Go on then, tell me about her. Is she the next Mrs Greenberg?"

Aaron had been married once before, a short-lived, tempestuous relationship which had ended when his bride of six months decided she wanted to volunteer abroad helping wildlife for the rest of her life. He didn't speak about it much. Eric hadn't known Aaron then, but from what he gathered, Aaron had been deeply hurt at the time.

Aaron looked scandalised. "Oi, give me a chance. We've only had the one date. It was nice."

He got a dreamy look on his face and Eric bit back a chuckle. He'd had his reservations about Aaron's crazy, well-meaning grandma arranging a date but it seemed to have worked out.

Eric patted Aaron on the back, putting a sad look on his face. "Mate, if your bubbie has anything to say about it, she's already got the wedding china picked out."

He laughed at the alarmed expression crossing Aaron's face and motioned toward the truck. "Come on. We're ready to rock and roll. Let's go see what lies in store for us today."

"My mam's just got a tummy ache. Can't you just give her some painkillers and be done with it? What the fuck are you waiting around for?"

The baleful glare of the twenty-something-year-old hovering over Eric as he tended to his patient was beginning to rattle him. The young girl had been blabbering on for over five minutes while he was trying to listen to the older woman's heartbeat and pulse.

They'd answered a 999 call for someone who'd collapsed, which had led them to the house in the middle of Tower Hamlets. Entering the grimy premises of the concrete, mass produced apartment on the tenth floor, an older woman had been supine on the floor as a younger one paced around the room, muttering to herself.

He'd known right away the young woman was tripping on something.

Eric took a deep breath. "Your mam hasn't got a stomach ache. She's got a burst appendix and we need to get her to the hospital as soon as possible. Could you please stand back and give me room?"

He waved the unkempt and unwashed girl back. What he didn't expect was the mouthful of spit he got in return. The glob landed on his cheek and he looked up, trying to control his temper, which burned quicker these days.

"Lady, that really wasn't necessary." What he wanted to say was, *Get the fuck out of my face before I give you a syringe of something you won't want, you little bitch.* "I'm only trying to help your mother." He glanced around for Aaron, who'd gone to fetch the board from the truck. "We're taking her to the hospital. She's in a bad way."

"She needs painkillers, you fucker. Not hospital. Who's gonna look after my kids when they come home from school if she's not here?" The wild-eyed girl was definitely on something from the spit surrounding her mouth and the frantic, twitching movements of her body. "And I'm nobody's lady. My name is Jessie."

You're right about that, he thought. *"Lady" is not a word I'd use to describe you.*

A prickle of alarm threaded its way down his spine. Tweakers, at the best of times, were dangerous, but this one looked right on the edge; probably why she was insisting on the painkillers. He had no doubt that, if they had been given, the woman lying on the floor wouldn't have seen any of them.

Eric breathed a sigh of relief when the chunky figure of his partner wheeled in the board.

"Aaron. Help me get her onto the board. We need to get her to the nearest hospital A-sap. I'll call in a blue once we're on the road." A blue call meant radioing ahead to the hospital to ensure someone would be waiting ready to take in their patient.

Aaron wasted no time. Within a few minutes, the unconscious woman was strapped to the board, ready to be transported.

As they wheeled her to the door, Jessie stood in front of it.

"You're not taking my mam anywhere, you tossers. Not until you give me the painkillers." She made a grab for the bag Aaron had on his shoulder.

He shouted and held it tight. "What do you think you're doing? Keep your hands off. This woman is going to the hospital, so I suggest you move away and let us do our job."

The knife appeared out of nowhere.

Dull light glinted off the blade Jessie held in her left hand. Both Eric and Aaron stopped. Eric glanced down at the patient, whose breathing was shallow, sweat beading across her forehead.

It wasn't the first time he and Aaron had been threatened, but a knife pointed at them scared him every time.

Aaron's eyes watched the knife warily. "Do you know how many patients we see who have their own knife turned against themselves? Put the damn thing down, lady."

Eric raised his hands, trying to placate the unstable woman before them. He thought he knew how to jolt her into letting them go.

"Jessie, put that the fuck down," he said quietly. "It's not going to do your mam any good if you hurt either of us or yourself. She's going to die if we don't get her to the hospital soon. Is that what you want? No one to look after your kids, pay your way and let you get on with what you want to do? You'll have to find a job. Maybe let your kids go into care. Is that your plan?"

No doubt the old woman on the board was the sole source of income and babysitting.

Jessie's eyes glittered as she contemplated Eric's argument. A sly smile crossed her face and she cocked her head. "Ya know, I guess you're right. Mam needs to get better and come back 'ere. I'll get me tablets elsewhere seeing as how you two are so bloody stingy with 'em." She waved the knife in their direction. "Go on, then Mr Hero. Get her to the hospital. She'd better make it or I'll come looking for you."

Aaron grunted. "Yeah, and we're both shuddering in our boots. Come on, pal. Let's get this sick woman to hospital where she belongs."

His follow-up, *And get her help to stay the hell away from you*, was unspoken but Eric knew his partner. Any chance he got to report this tweaker and keep the old woman safe, he'd take it, as would Eric.

Aaron cursed as they wheeled the board toward the truck. "Shit. I hate people like that. Freeloaders thinking the world owes them a living. Using their parents to support a drug habit. Thinking violence solves everything."

They loaded the patient into the truck. Eric sighed. "Yeah. It takes all sorts. I guess we'd better report the situation, let Social Services take a look at the kids. I'm not a fan of them, but this case warrants it."

Eric drove carefully, not wanting his patient to jolt around in the back and hurt more. The blue lights were flashing and traffic allowed them easy access.

An hour later they delivered their patient and made their reports to the hospital and Social Services. The prognosis was bleak. They might be able to do something with the kids but the grandmother was another matter. It would be her decision whether to go back to her daughter, or not.

Aaron and Eric got back in the truck in the car park and looked at each other. The radio was silent. Eric breathed a sigh of relief, knowing it would be short-lived. He needed some distracting.

"Tell me more about this lady of yours," he asked idly as he watched his partner complete paperwork. "I don't even know her name."

Aaron looked up. "Her name is Leah. She's twenty-five and works as a paralegal for a company just outside London. She's smart, and she makes me laugh." He gave a self- deprecating sniff. "And she likes short, cuddly men with meat on them, so I'm the ideal man for her."

"You going on another date then?" Eric gazed out the window, watching people walk by.

Aaron shrugged. "I asked her if she wanted to go to a film and she said yes. We need to sort out which one. I think she likes the same ones I do—horror and thrillers, not those horrible rom-com things."

"Oh, she's a keeper all right," Eric said drily. "Hold onto her, mate. Anyone who likes your type of gore is definitely the woman for you."

"Talking about my love life— you still haven't told me much about this new man of yours." Aaron winked. "You came in this morning with a spring in your step. Are you gonna see him again then?"

Eric shrugged. "I guess. Kyle is good fun, and we get on well." In his mind that translated into, *He's smoking hot and I'm really into him*, but he wasn't telling his nosy partner that. In the past, if he'd been even marginally interested in a guy, Aaron had seemed to make it his life's mission to push him into a committed relationship. Aaron knew most of the story about Lincoln and believed Eric needed another warm body in his bed to get over his grief.

His best friend Deke felt much the same way. He was always trying to convince Chrissy to set Eric up on dates with random guys. He hadn't been a priest; he'd had a few sexual exploits since Linc died, but Eric hadn't found someone he really liked. Until now.

Aaron stared at him, eyes narrowed. "You're not telling me everything," he growled. "There's something about this guy. Kyle's special to you. I can feel it."

Eric stared back innocently. "You're not your bubbie, partner," he chuckled. "Don't have me married off like she wants you to be. I'm quite happy with the status quo." For now, he admitted silently. He certainly wasn't averse to things getting a little more serious.

Before Aaron could respond, the radio crackled again with another callout. His partner grunted as Eric started the engine and pulled away from the parking lot. "Maybe we need a double date.

You and your man and me and Leah." Aaron's face brightened at that prospect.

Eric shuddered. The last thing he wanted to do was introduce Kyle to an inquisitive Aaron. The two men potentially chatting together gave Eric hives. Who knew what might be revealed in the heat of a relaxed or drunken moment. Aaron knew a lot of embarrassing stories Eric would rather not have revealed.

"Sounds good," he lied as he raced down the road toward their next emergency. "It'll need to wait until I get back from France in a couple of weeks' time. I'm subbing for David at that camping trip at Verdon Gorge, remember?"

One of their paramedic friends, David, had broken a leg skiing in Austria a few weeks ago. He'd been desperate and Eric had agreed to fill in as one of the official medics on call at the camping lodge in France at the so-called Grand Canyon of Europe.

Fortuitously, David happened to be the son of the chief medic at Shoreditch, and strings had been pulled to enable Eric to go as part of his on-going training. He was looking forward to it as a working holiday with pay.

He groaned softly when he realised he hadn't mentioned it to Kyle. Then again, things weren't serious between them, and still too new. Kyle wouldn't be bothered if he went away. Would he?

"Oh, yeah, you're gadding off to Europe to spend time with the rich people," Aaron sniffed. "Leaving me to be paired up with that twat Rosie." He rolled his eyes and Eric grinned.

Ross "Rosie" Corkton was a beefy, hairy brute of a man, who constantly sweated in the truck and gave off a cheesy aroma that made them both gag. Rosie was also one heck of a medic.

"Aww," Eric teased as he glanced at his scowling friend. "You're gonna miss me. How cute."

"Don't get ahead of yourself. I won't miss your sorry arse," Aaron growled. He held on tight as Eric took a corner sharply, avoiding a bicycle courier that had darted out in front of them.

"Stupid tosser," Aaron yelled out of the open window. "You want to be travelling with us then? First-class accommodation in the back, you knucklehead."

Eric sniggered. Aaron certainly had a way with words.

At least the incident had made him forget the double date.

Eric's mobile rang as he was walking down the path to his front door. He grinned when he saw who it was, his spirits instantly lifting.

"Kyle. Hey there. This is a pleasant surprise."

"Yeah." There was the sound of retching and he frowned.

"You okay? You sound sick."

"I am." Kyle's voice was muffled. "I went out today and grabbed a quick doner kebab from a food cart and now I'm fucking puking my guts up." There was another awful sound as Eric fumbled to get his door open.

"You want me to come over and play medic?" he asked as he threw his keys onto the dining table. "I know it's late, but I'm happy to do it." His shift had finished half an hour ago. It was almost eleven pm.

"Oh shit, I'm so sorry." Kyle's voice was panicked. "I've been in bed all afternoon, and didn't realise how late it was. Fuck, I'm a complete plonker…"

"Hey, don't sweat it. You were obviously out of it. Are you sure you don't want me to check you out?" Kyle's tired chuckle made Eric's chest fluttery.

"You know, any other time the chance to get you to play medic and come to check me over would be a resounding yes. But right now, I'm a mess, all barfed out and I just want to get into bed with my bucket. I'll take a rain check though."

"Um, okay." He still wasn't sure why Kyle had called. "Did you need me for anything else?"

The muffled expletive on the other side of the phone made him laugh softly. "Yeah, I was supposed to pass on a message from Ryan for you much earlier but I forgot. Hence the late night call. When he sent me home, saying, and I quote, 'You looked sicker than a goat on fucking crack', he asked if it was possible to remind you about coming around to the club tomorrow before your shift? Apparently, you're going to be a witness for him on some business thingy. He's out somewhere this evening where he has no mobile signal or he'd have called to remind you himself."

Eric had forgotten about that. "Sure. My shift starts at ten, but I'll pop over a bit before then."

"Cool. Okay, I'm going back to bed to puke over my sheets and feel sorry for myself. And before you start on me, I have some boiled ginger ale, a packet of crackers and some anti-nausea pills. I'm all set."

"Hmm. That's a start. Call me in the morning, let me know how you are."

"Ahh, you care 'bout me. That's so sweet." Unfortunately, Kyle's cute sentiment was spoiled by another bout of vomiting. "Yuck, gotta go. The porcelain beckons."

The line went dead. Eric put down his phone and stared at it worriedly. Kyle sounded terrible. What they had was still new, but the last thing Eric wanted to do was be overprotective and scare Kyle away. The man had a stubborn streak that'd piss a mule off. If he said he didn't want company, fine.

Tomorrow when he rang, Eric would see if he could get another date for them to meet up again before…fuck. He still hadn't said anything to Kyle about the upcoming France trip.

Tomorrow, he promised. *I'll let him know then when we speak.*

Unfortunately, Eric didn't get the chance to speak to Kyle before Eric left two days later. Knee-deep in amniotic fluid delivering a pair of twin girls at the time, he'd missed Kyle's call the next afternoon explaining in detail that he felt much better.

After the babies, Eric and Aaron's other call-outs hadn't been as rewarding and were doubly demanding. Over the next two days, London seemed to go crazy. They treated a man with a suspected heart attack, which turned out to be chest pains because he'd taken too much Viagra. They attended two student suicides at a local University, both heart-breaking and sobering. Drug overdoses were rife, as were stabbings. And when they called on an old man with dementia, he was dehydrated and delirious with pain from a beating by a gang of youths. When he saw Aaron, the poor man thought Aaron was his son, and Eric's heart had broken.

In between this were the usual 999 calls that should have been referred to doctors and night clinics.

Already exhausted, disheartened, depressed and grumpy from lack of sleep—more nightmares had kept him up at night—when the time came for Eric to get on the plane to France, he'd sighed with relief.

His inner voice whispered, *I'm sure he's not going to miss me. He doesn't need me being all moody in his life. I'm bad company right now.*

Chapter Nine

Kyle wasn't at work pining over the fact he hadn't heard from Eric in a couple of days. He definitely fucking *wasn't*.

His last message telling Eric he was feeling better had been unanswered. He didn't even know if he'd read it. Not for the first time, Kyle wished he'd used Messenger or WhatsApp so he could tell.

He'd been tempted to call, but a streak of bloody-mindedness had crept in, a little voice whispering that perhaps Eric didn't want to be contacted. That he wasn't interested anymore.

Damn his insecurities. Kyle scowled and kicked the floor moulding moodily. Then he formed his mouth into a fake smile and knocked once on Ryan's door before he opened it, then entered.

He had a job to do on pain of death from a positively scary man.

Ryan smiled up at him from his desk. "Hey, everything okay out there? Need me for anything?"

Kyle kept the smile on his face. "Nope. All under control, boss. How are you feeling?"

Ryan shrugged. "I'm fine and dandy. Chomping at the bit to get back to work without a bunch of fucking nursemaids watching my every move."

Kyle grinned for real now. He sat down on the corner of Ryan's desk. "Ooh, full-blown bitch alert. Isn't it nearly your bedtime?"

Mango had insisted Ryan be home by ten every night as part of his recovery. Kyle was Mango's unwilling accomplice.

Ryan narrowed his eyes. "Fuck. You."

It was only nine pm.

Kyle sniggered. "Not my rules, boss. Them be Mango's commands." He peered over the desk down at Ryan's legs. They were covered with black chinos but Kyle knew what had been under them until a few days ago. "At least those awful stockings have gone," he drawled, fanning his face like a Southern belle. "I do declare, sir, such a shade of puce I never did see on a gentleman of your standing."

Ryan chuckled. "Shut up, you." He bowed his head in acknowledgement. "Thank fuck they've gone. I hated wearing them. Such passion killers."

"How are things…down there?" Kyle waved in the direction of Ryan's groin.

In a weak moment, Ryan had confided that the medication he was on had caused some technical issues in sustaining an erection. The doctor had said it was normal and would resolve itself over time but Kyle knew Ryan was mortified it had happened.

"Getting better," Ryan said. "It helps the medication is now maintenance only and not as high a dose as it was. I'll be able to give it up for good in a week or so, I hope."

Mango will be helping you get it up tonight, Kyle thought wickedly. He's not going to let you off easy. Get you off, more likely.

He nodded, trying to keep the smirk off his face. "You've been through a lot, Ryan. And you came out with flying colours. Not many aftereffects, a clean bill of health, apart from the check-ups. You're a lucky man."

"I am," Ryan acknowledged. "I give thanks every day for coming through it like I did."

Kyle nodded and looked at his watch. "It's time to leave the office, boss. Mango asked me to get you home a bit earlier."

Ryan frowned. "Why?"

Kyle tried to keep the glee out of his voice. He knew exactly what was going on. He'd helped Mango pick out the outfit for Ryan, who was going to look so damned hot in it.

"Dunno. He told me to kick my boss out at nine o'clock sharp or he'd come down and get you himself."

Ryan swore but he stood, looking for his suit jacket. "Damn man is a pain in my arse."

"Isn't that the whole point?" Kyle smirked. "Have you seen Eric lately? He hasn't been around since he came in a while ago."

Or since we had a breathless, heavenly frot at my place.

Ryan shook his head. "No, he's away for a couple of weeks. He went backpacking with some friends in the Grand Canyon, I think."

Kyle's stomach clenched, his chest constricting.

Eric went away to the US and didn't even bother to let me know? Bastard. A text would have sufficed.

He forced himself to stay calm. "Oh. That sounds cool. Well, you'd better get going before that boyfriend of yours comes down and drags you away."

He shooed Ryan out of the office and watched him climb the stairs to his flat. Once he was out of sight, Kyle went into the office and closed the door. He stood, shoulders bowed, staring out of the window.

Kyle sat nursing his drink, staring at the frenzied hordes of hopeful gamblers surrounding him. He'd come down to the Hippodrome Casino in the West End in the hopes it would lift him out of his doldrums. So far all it had done was get him tipsy and make his hands itch to take over from the croupier and earn himself some money at the craps table.

He watched idly as the dealer shuffled the cards and dealt another losing punter his hand.

"So, are you going to drink that or just glare around the room looking sexy?" The lilting Jamaican voice made Kyle look up as a rather attractive black man, perhaps a few years older, sat down next to him. Tall, clean-shaven and dressed in a deep blue suit with a light yellow shirt and matching tie, he looked made for the cover of a fashion magazine. Then the man grinned, making him look even more delicious.

Kyle looked down at the whisky he'd been nursing. "I'm drinking it, just making it last. This place isn't cheap." *Shit, now he's going to think I'm asking him to buy me a drink.*

Sure enough, Jamaica laughed. "Then, my friend, I shall buy you another while you finish that one." He gestured to a passing waitress who swished over and took the order.

Kyle panicked. He didn't tend to take drinks from strange men in casinos. He'd learnt his lesson a long time ago on that one.

"No, shit, that wasn't a hint to buy me a drink. Honestly, I'm fine with this one."

"Nonsense. I insist. A beautiful man like you deserves it."

Kyle frowned. "It's a little risqué to go around paying that type of compliment to strange men in places like this. How do you know I wouldn't pop you one in the nose for trying to come onto me?" He squinted through slightly hazy eyes. Crap, the whisky was starting to go to his head with mega force now.

The man reached out a hand. Kyle shook it, and was engulfed in warm skin and firm fingers. "My name is Louis Devon Thomas. Now we are no longer strangers, Mr Violet Eyes. Now please, could you return the favour by giving me your name?"

"My name is Kyle. And my question still stands."

Louis inclined his head graciously. "You work at Club Delish. I live in this area and frequent it often. I have seen you there. I didn't expect to see you here on a busy Friday night. From what I have seen of you, you are always working. Imagine my delight when I saw you sitting here. Alone."

Kyle's insides constricted and a chill fingered up a spine.

Louis must have seen the flash of panic because he leaned back and shook his head. "I promise you, I'm no stalker. This is a coincidence, nothing more. You have nothing to fear from me."

Kyle's face flushed. "Sorry, I'm being paranoid. Ignore me."

Louis frowned. "I will do no such thing. I saw fear in your eyes just now. You are quite right to question my intentions."

Wow, that's unexpected. Someone who doesn't think I'm a freak.

Kyle toyed with his glass.

"You are not with anyone here tonight?" Louis glanced idly around the busy venue.

Kyle shook his head. "No, the man I'm seeing—or was seeing—disappeared without saying goodbye. I'm on my own."

Shit, way to bear your soul to a stranger, arsehole.

And it wasn't quite true. A week ago Kyle had received a text from Eric saying, "Sorry, forgot to mention I was going away. Will catch up with you when I get back." Then there'd been another text with a photo of a shirtless Eric—looking goddamned tanned and sexy—smiling next to some big-breasted blonde woman in a bikini with the caption "Wish you were here."

Kyle hadn't liked that text one little bit. Not the woman bit anyway.

Louis's eyes brightened. "*Were* seeing? So, you aren't together anymore? I stand a chance?" He had an amused and kind face, and Kyle thought he could really like this man and his gentle demeanour.

He shrugged. "I'm not sure. I thought maybe I scared him away somehow." His tone was wistful.

Louis leaned in. "You like this man very much. He is special to you, yes?"

Kyle started to say no then shut his mouth. He sighed. "I think he could be."

Louis stared at him. "Then I shall not hit on another man's significant other until I am sure there are no emotional attachments. Your man does not know how lucky he is to have you."

Kyle looked down at his empty glass. He wasn't used to compliments. Quite the contrary.

Faggot. Dirty sinner. Cocktease. Mario's hissed words echoed in Kyle's head.

The waitress arrived with their drinks and Louis took them, and offered one to Kyle. "We shall drink as friends and I will sit here hoping that the next time I see you, you are truly alone." He raised his drink. "But somehow I think I am not going to be that fortunate. Cheers." He raised his drink and Kyle clinked his own against the glass.

"Thanks," Kyle said softly. "You seem like a decent bloke. Maybe under different circumstances…"

Louis chuckled. "I won't hold my breath. But it is nice to know."

They drank in comfortable silence.

"I used to work in a casino in Las Vegas," Kyle finally broke the silence. "Much bigger than this one. I did that"—he gestured over to the croupier dealing cards—"along with working the bar sometimes, handling the cash and the back office. It was a lot of fun but your time is never your own. I think I used to get three to four hours a day to myself, max, because of the shifts I worked."

Louis leaned forward curiously. "Las Vegas? That must have been incredible. Why are you here now then instead of there? If I were still a gambler, I would never leave such a place." He made a moue then gave a self-deprecating chuckle. "I would probably die there, either from forgetting to eat, or drinking too much while I play the tables. Or some mobster would decide I owe him money and to teach me a lesson." His face darkened and Kyle saw the shadow in his eyes. "Vegas is not the right place for me."

"I saw those men," Kyle admitted. "The ones with a fever in their eyes and hunger in the bellies to spin yet another wheel or pull another slot machine, or turn over another hand of cards. It's an addiction that's tough to resist."

Louis nodded. "I understand it well. I was one of them. But when I realised how badly I let it control my life, I joined Gamblers Anonymous and it has been four years since I played a table, or held a deck of cards."

Kyle's eyes widened. "Then why come to a place like this? Isn't the temptation too great?"

Louis laughed. "That's like asking a man who has given up drinking whether he can walk into a pub without succumbing. No, I choose to remind myself of how I ruined my life the first time around by coming in here. It tells me what I have achieved so far has been worth it." He flashed a grin at Kyle. "And it allows me to make new friends."

They clicked glasses again.

"You never did answer my original question about why you left there," Louis said musingly. "If you do not wish to say, then please, tell me to mind my own business."

Kyle had no intention of telling anyone why he'd left. Instead he shrugged and put on a blank face. "I got tired of the glitz and glamour and never having any time to myself. I moved back to the U.K. to have an easier life, and I love it here. I'm settled now."

"I see." Louis nodded thoughtfully. "Then we shall leave that as the explanation."

Louis knew there was more to Kyle's leaving than that. Damn, the man was perceptive.

Kyle's mobile vibrated in his pocket and he smiled apologetically. "Let me just get this. It's probably my friend Lucinda. She was going to meet me here after her night out."

He checked the voice message on his phone. Sure enough, it was from Luce. "Hey, London, I'm not gonna make it." Her voice was slurred yet happy. "I met up with this sexy lady who wants to fly me to Paris—don't worry, I know her, she's no stranger—so we're on our way to the airfield now." She giggled. "Oops, sorry, Lanie. Didn't mean to spill my drink on you." There was a soft murmur and Luce burst into a peal of laughter. "Wow, that's just, I don't know what to say. Maybe wait until we're on the plane instead of the taxi?"

There was a crackle and a sound Kyle really didn't want to interpret. It was wet, sloppy and reeked of sexual activity of some sort. Kissing, he hoped. Then Luce's voice spoke again, dreamy and far away. "Anyway, have fun and I'll talk to you when I get back, whenever that it is. Love you, baby."

The message ended. Sighing, Kyle put his phone back into his pocket and met Louis's enquiring gaze. "She's flying to Paris," he murmured. "From the sounds of it, she's having fun."

Louis's eyes gleamed in satisfaction. "Then I have you all to myself for the night. Shall we get another drink?"

Kyle thought he might as well. It was only eleven and he wasn't ready to go home yet. Eric wasn't waiting in his bed so what the fuck did he have to lose?

"Yep, let's do this. Except this is my round. I don't expect to be a kept man."

Oh God, and now he was flirting.

Louis laughed loudly. "Kyle, I am quite sure of it. Yes, you can buy me a cocktail. A hanky-panky if you please."

Kyle hooted with mirth. "One hanky-panky coming up. Although there'll be none of that tonight." He cast a mock glare at Louis who collapsed in amusement.

"Ah, we shall see about that. I am sure we can put our minds to mischief if we think about it."

As Kyle motioned the waiter over, he felt a warm glow inside. Tonight was turning out to be rather pleasant after all. Making new friends wasn't so tough.

A week later, Kyle was in Club Delish helping Ryan take in a new alcohol order. They held their respective stock sheets and ticked off the deliveries one by one. It was a cool day outside but inside the bar it was warm. Sweat trickled down Kyle's back as he stood there.

As usual, Ryan looked completely in control and effortlessly together. The man didn't even have a sheen of perspiration on his face, unlike Kyle who'd rolled up his shirtsleeves and untucked his shirt to let air circulate around his body

"Are you looking forward to Eric coming back tomorrow?" Ryan raised an eyebrow at Kyle, who scowled.

"Oh, did he go away? I hadn't noticed." Kyle turned and placed his stock sheet on the bar as he studied it without seeing. He hadn't had any other texts since the last one of Eric with the busty blonde.

Ryan sniggered. "You've been like a bear whose favourite twink has been taken away, darling. Don't try to fool me. Delilah knows better."

Kyle's face burned. *Am I that transparent? Oh, yeah. This is Ryan.*

"I don't really care whether he's back or not," Kyle declared loftily. "I met some really nice guy at the casino the other night and we've been hanging out. Eric coming back is neither here nor there."

He and Louis had been seeing each other as friends. They'd been to a film and dinner at Galileo's, where Kyle had met the famous and oh-so-cute head chef Eddie. Kyle loved men with red hair and Eddie had been adorable. And from the way Gideon, the restaurant owner, kept a predatory eye on him, he obviously thought so too.

Ryan sidled up to him. "Liar," he said softly. He reached out a hand as if to pat Kyle's arm then pulled it back.

"You don't have to do that," Kyle muttered. "You can touch me if you want to."

Ryan narrowed his eyes. "You seem a little skittish around people who touch you. I don't want to make you feel uncomfortable."

"I'm only uncomfortable with guys who seem…threatening." Kyle couldn't meet Ryan's eyes in case he saw the shame there. "My friends don't count among them."

Ryan growled. Actually, growled. "I knew someone had done a number on you. If you ever want to talk about it, you know I'm here." He gave Kyle an awkward pat on the back then turned to finish his stock count. Kyle was relieved beyond measure Ryan hadn't pushed the issue, and had simply given an offer of support.

"Thanks," Kyle said gruffly and picked up another lengthy stock sheet. They had a lot to go through before the club opened tonight. Wednesday night was Leather Night and they were expecting quite a crowd.

Later that evening, sandwiched between two muscle-bound leather daddies making out on the floor as Kyle tried to navigate back to the bar and check on the stock and general goings-on, he spotted a familiar figure talking to Ryan in a quieter spot of the club.

Eric was back. Kyle's stomach fluttered and he couldn't stop the tingle that spread through his body at seeing his wayward paramedic. He ignored the flush of warmth and pretended he hadn't seen Eric. Kyle knew he was being childish, but he couldn't help it.

His plans were thwarted when someone shouted his name across the floor.

"Kyle." Dammit. "Eric's here. Do you want to say hello?" Kyle scowled at Ryan, whose face shone with glee. Or perhaps Mr Always Perfectly Groomed had sweat on his face, Kyle thought uncharitably. He'd no option but to turn and make his way toward the pair.

Eric looked amazing. Tanned, chestnut hair curly, and he was wearing a white cut-off vest with tight black jeans. The man looked edible enough to eat right there. Kyle wanted to bite the face off the young man behind Eric eyeing him with a distinct look of appreciation and lust.

Mine, he wanted to growl. *All mine.* Fuck off. And yet he had no idea whether Eric was his or not.

Getting closer, he swore inwardly. Crap. Ryan was as impeccable as ever, no trace of perspiration.

Eric smiled uncertainly. "Hey, Kyle. How are you doing?"

Kyle waved a purple-tipped hand airily. "Oh, I'm good. Out and about."

Eric nodded. "That's good. Good." He cleared his throat and glanced around.

Kyle couldn't resist it. "I thought you weren't coming back until tomorrow? At least, that's what someone told me. I didn't know first-hand of course."

His snarky comment had a visible effect on both Eric and Ryan. Ryan snorted with laughter and turned around with a flap of his hand. "I'm going to leave you bitches to sort things out. See ya." He disappeared into the throng.

Eric, however, looked shamefaced. "Yeah, 'bout that. I'm sorry I didn't call but where we were had a bad signal. We had satellite phones up on the mountain, but personal calls weren't really allowed."

Kyle reached up and ran a hand through his hair, trying to look nonchalant. "Oh, don't bother to explain. I understand…wait. What do you mean they didn't allow you personal calls? I thought you were on holiday in the US?"

Eric gaped at him. "The US? No, I was in France for work. I was in a remote holiday spot on a private estate filling in for a friend of mine who broke his leg. Why did you think I was in America?"

"Ryan said you were backpacking in the Grand Canyon. I assumed that was the US?

Eric laughed. "Ah, that would be because I was at Verdon Gorge. It's called the Grand Canyon of Europe. Ryan must have got confused."

Kyle felt a little stupid, but still riled. "I had no idea there was another one in bloody France."

"And I wasn't backpacking." Eric explained. "Not in the true sense. I was a medic up there in one of the fancy retreats run by some billionaire bloke. The guests all go off hiking and skiing, and they like a medic or two on call. It's good work, well paid, so I took it when my mate David couldn't go. He broke his leg."

"Oh." Kyle wasn't sure what to say. It seemed a reasonable something for Eric to do given his day job, and perhaps Kyle had judged Eric too harshly. He'd been out saving lives after all. How could Kyle stay annoyed with him?

Eric reached out with a soft smile and caressed Kyle's cheek. "Did you get my texts? I managed to get away to the town for a little bit when we picked up supplies. Signal wasn't great but I managed to get to the top of the mountain nearby. Thought I'd let you know I was okay."

"Oh, I could see that," Kyle said. "The picture of you with the full-breasted lady was a nice touch. I thought you might have changed sides."

"Someone jealous?" Eric's eyes darkened and Kyle's knees weakened.

Kyle huffed. "No. We don't have a claim on each other. I don't care what you do when you're away." He turned to the barman and asked for a snakebite shot. He needed it.

"I think you do," Eric said with a grin. "That full-breasted lady was the wife of the owner of the resort. Happily married as well."

"Whatever." Kyle knocked back the shot the barman had pushed over to him.

Eric snorted. "No, not jealous at all," he remarked. Then his face shadowed. "Listen, I'm sorry I didn't tell you before I went that I was going away. Things at work got hairy. It was pretty stressful and before I knew it, I was on the plane." He gave a wry grimace. "I wasn't really good company at the time so I didn't think you'd want to hear from me being all depressed."

Kyle motioned for another drink and looked at Eric. "You want anything?"

Eric nodded and Kyle ordered two snakebites.

"Is that the real reason you didn't tell me you were going away?" he snapped. "Because you feared my sensibilities may take offence at the fact you'd had a bad day and felt shitty and you'd taint me with it?"

Eric blinked. "Yeah, I suppose...I wouldn't have put it that way, but yeah, I guess so."

"Well, perhaps next time you can stop thinking I'm some sort of blushing virgin and let me know you're out of town for two weeks, Mister." Kyle's tone rose a faction as he went into drama mode.

Shit. He'd just done exactly what he'd said he wasn't going to. He'd staked a claim on the man. He downed his shot in frustration and slammed it on the bar.

Eric watched him through shuttered eyes, reaching for him and pressing their bodies together. The hard ridge in Eric's pants nudged Kyle's.

"That was the hottest thing I've ever seen—you getting all toppy on my arse." Eric murmured in Kyle's ear.

Kyle opened his mouth to say he absolutely wasn't, and found it filled with tongue. His lips were taken in a kiss that made his cock harder and sent thrills through his body he imagined were akin to being shocked by a pulse of warm electricity.

He heard a moan and was mortified to find out it was him. Eric lavished attention on his mouth as if were the tastiest thing he'd ever eaten. Kyle was thoroughly enjoying being the dish of the day. Dimly he was aware that he was making out during his work shift in the middle of Ryan's club, but he didn't care.

Warm hands slid under his shirt and sent ripples of fire down his skin and straight into his groin. Waves of desire and need spread like warm smoke through his body and he knew if he didn't stop this, he was going to come in his pants.

That would not be a good public look for the house manager of Club Delish. Ryan would castrate him.

Reluctantly, he pulled away, regretting the loss of Eric's hungry mouth the second he did. "I'm still mad with you. And I'm supposed to be working, not fucking about on the dance floor."

"Then maybe later I can fuck you *on* the floor." Eric trailed a finger across Kyle's swollen and wet lips.

Kyle wanted to melt into a puddle of goo simply at the prospect of his promised debauchery. "Oh God, you can't say things like to me here."

He rejoiced as he looked down to see yes, his silk tuxedo jacquard jacket was covering most of his excited groin from view.

Eric slid a hand across Kyle's cock, his eyes dark and liquid. "I can if it gets you to not be mad with me." He squeezed and bent down for another kiss.

Kyle stepped back, noticing the bartender's amused grin along with other patrons who watched them like sharks scenting blood. He had no doubt if he turned around and snapped his fingers right then, he'd have a horde of them begging to be the meat in a Kyle and Eric sandwich.

"No," he said as firmly as he could muster, given his aroused state. "This isn't happening right now. If you really want to apologise to me, you can pick me up after work so I don't have to navigate the tube to yours and take me back to your place. I get off at two." *Only four more hours to go.* "Then we can look at the whole 'fuck on the floor' scenario. If you're not too tired, that is."

"Oh, I'll be fine," Eric drawled, his eyes darting to something behind Kyle. "Not sure you'll make it though." He began to laugh softly.

Kyle turned and looked right into icy blue eyes that bore into his brain like a drill.

"Having fun, are we?" Ryan purred and Kyle's stomach roiled. Delilah was making an appearance. "I confess, I thought I was clear when I said in my job interviews my employees should set an example on the club floor and not commence fucking in plain sight."

"We weren't actually fucking," Kyle said piteously, "We were just—"

Ryan waved a finger. "Tut-tut. It was certainly fucking—of the mouth."

Kyle looked into the crowd, his hard-on now shrivelled to nothing in the face of Ryan's—or was it Delilah's? Sometimes the two were indistinguishable—wilting glare.

"Now, Kyle darling." Ryan's silky voice was both dangerous and teasing. "Do you think you could get back to work and leave your sexual liaisons until you get off at twelve?"

He opened his mouth to say his shift didn't end until two am and shut it promptly at the amused glint in Ryan's eyes. *God, I have the best boss and job ever.* "Yes, I can keep it in my pants until then. Eric, pick me up at twelve, okay? I'll meet you in the staff car park."

Ryan acknowledged Kyle with a regal tilt of his head then winked at Eric. Without a backward glance, in that way he had, he glided off toward the staircase to his office.

Kyle took a deep breath. "Well, that didn't go as badly as it could have. See you later then? I'd better get back to work before Ryan-Delilah really lets me have it."

"It's a date." Eric turned to go, his hair mussed and unruly where Kyle had run his hands through it. "And I look forward to the floor show." He grinned and Kyle's thoughts turned dark and raunchy. He suppressed them manfully.

"Let's hope I'm good enough a performer for you then. See you at twelve."

Kyle blew a kiss to Eric, turned and made his way to the front desk, rolling his eyes in despair at his easy submission into needy pushover.

Chapter Ten

God, that man is going to be the death of me. He kisses like sin.

Kyle's mouth was a sinful smorgasbord of sheer aggression and no-holds-barred tongue action, and for one moment Eric thought he might suffocate. The man knew how to work his body too. Every press of his against Eric's, every sneaky touch of his fingers on skin and the heat-inducing cock rubs against Eric's groin—God. Kyle had no idea how lethal he was to Eric's sanity.

Or maybe he did.

When Eric reached home and got into the shower, anxious to prepare for Kyle's visit, he reran his mental video to recall every moment of that kiss in exquisite detail. More than once his hands drifted down to his cock, which begged for release. He wasn't sure what was better—beating off in the shower to take the edge off, or waiting for Kyle to do it for him.

He settled on rubbing one out, knowing that if he got inside Kyle in his current state Eric would be likely to blow too soon. He wanted to seduce Kyle until he cried Eric's name, and then he would take his time sliding into Kyle as they enjoyed a leisurely session that made them both gasp and come their brains out.

Kyle deserved to be cherished, like a fine port.

Eric dressed in loose sweats and a long-sleeve tee-shirt to pick up Kyle. Eric drove his rarely used white 1972 MGB Roadster, nicknamed Little Lady, which was parked outside his house, ready to go. It had been a birthday present from his parents on his twenty-first birthday.

He'd already fixed the tonneau cover, thinking it was a bit too chilly to have the car's roof down.

He set out into the chilly night air. It might only be a few miles away, but London traffic could be a bitch any time of the night or day.

Eric got to the club just before twelve and parked behind the venue in a small car park reserved only for employees. Ryan had been gracious about letting him park Little Lady there, muttering something about fools with cars and their obsessions with scraps of smoke puking metal.

Eric wasn't even sure Ryan could drive, let alone whether he owned a car.

While he waited, Eric scrolled through his phone, glancing up now and then to check if Kyle was there. It wasn't a particularly savoury place to walk. The parking lot was dark and closed in, and against one wall there was a row of dumpsters.

Eric hated dumpsters. He'd once been called out to a scene to find the man in need of medical assistance had just beaten another human being to death and dumped her in a dumpster like garbage.

Eric had hated every minute of tending to his patient, a crude roughneck of a brute who'd had a major heart attack after his violent assault on a much younger woman, apparently his sister.

Aaron had taken one look inside the bin and shaken his head. There'd been no saving the beaten girl. The brute, however—that was another matter. He'd recovered to face murder charges and was now in prison.

"Why the hell are you thinking about this now, when you're about to go on a date with a sexy bloke?" Eric muttered to himself. "Think sexy thoughts."

He closed his eyes, took a deep breath then squeaked in panic when firm lips pressed against his with a low chuckle. His eyes shot open as the warm mouth left his.

"Are you meditating?" Kyle stood beside the open window, rucksack over his shoulder, jacket slung over his arm. He looked tired but happy. "Aligning your chakras, are we?" He grinned then walked around the front of the car to climb in the passenger seat. He muttered as he tried to stretch out his long legs. "I love the wheels, but she isn't Kyle friendly." He glanced across at Eric. "You look as if you fit, so how come I feel like a sardine?"

"Practice," Eric assured him as he started the car. "I'd suggest you keep your bag on your lap as there isn't room for it in the back."

Finally, Kyle settled in with his seat belt fastened and bag on lap as instructed. Eric pulled out of the dim parking lot and soon they were on the street.

"Thanks for coming to fetch me," Kyle murmured as he rested, half asleep, against the chair back. "I wasn't sure how far away you lived, and after a shift like tonight, I'd have fallen asleep and missed my stop."

Eric placed a hand on Kyle's thigh. "No problem. I love an excuse to get Little Lady out and drive her."

"Little Lady?" Kyle chuckled. "I like it."

Watching Kyle fall asleep was like watching a kid snuggle in under a comforter. He tucked in against the side of the door, hugging his bag possessively. He wore a small smile with those full lips slightly parted. His chest rose and fell evenly under his light pink shirt and a strand of dark purple hair fell across his cheek.

Eric wanted to brush it off but was scared he'd wake up Kyle. This man seemed to bring out all Eric's protective instincts—something he'd last felt with Lincoln.

"He reminds me of you, Linc," Eric whispered in the quiet confines of the car. "Strong on the outside, vulnerable on the inside. Mouthy and too damn sexy for his own good."

He could almost hear Lincoln's chuckle and reply. *You have a type, Eric-bear. Just remember he's not me. I'm gone. You need to find someone new.*

The thought brought a lump to Eric's throat and he was glad when he saw his house and pulled into his parking space. He switched off the engine and looked at Kyle, who slumbered on. It seemed a pity to wake him but he couldn't leave him here squashed in the car.

"Come on, Sleeping Beauty." Eric brushed his fingers down Kyle's bristled cheek. "We're here."

Kyle's eyes opened blearily and then he shot up, staring around him. "Oh, shit. I fell asleep, didn't I? I'm so sorry. Some late-night booty call this is."

Eric stared at him. "Booty call? That's not what this is about, is it? Because that wasn't my intention…"

Kyle swiftly shut him up by pressing cool lips to his. "Hush. It was a figure of speech." He opened his car door and clambered out, stretching and giving a low groan of satisfaction. "Shit, I feel like one of those jack-in-the-boxes that's just popped out."

His tee-shirt drew up and Eric's breath hitched at the glimpse of Kyle's lean, naked torso and the treasure trail leading down, disappearing in his low-slung formal trousers.

"Come on, let's get inside," Eric said gruffly.

Kyle yawned and followed him inside like a lanky puppy. Eric reached up and switched on the light.

Kyle blinked. "Wow, nice. Very white and minimalist. Does the kitchen actually get used?"

Eric frowned. "Well, yeah, of course it does. I don't like stuff being out looking untidy, so it's all packed away until I want to use it. Same for the rest of the place." His home was a simple, clean, white and cream layout, an open-plan kitchen and lounge with two bedrooms to the rear.

Kyle nodded, seemingly fascinated by Eric's lack of ornaments or décor. Apart from his Michael Thompsett prints on the walls, Eric wasn't keen on *stuff* littering his place.

Kyle dropped his bag and bounded over to the long, chenille couch, bouncing on it as he lay down. His face assumed an expression of bliss. Eric despaired whether he was ever going to get to take Kyle to bed tonight. The man looked hell bound to fall asleep.

"This is really comfy." Kyle gave a moan of enjoyment.

Eric sighed and went to the small bar cabinet. "Do you fancy a drink before you go to sleep?" He pulled down the bar top and considered what he had in there. Whisky would do, he knew Kyle enjoyed it.

"Who said anything about sleeping?" came an unexpected murmur in his ear, followed by a warm lick.

Heart thudding, Eric turned to face a smirking and obviously unrepentant Kyle. "You have to stop doing that." Eric exclaimed. "You're going to kill me. And how the hell do you manage to creep up on people so silently?"

Kyle shrugged. "It's a knack." He ran a finger down Eric's jawline, eyes sparkling. "Can I take a quick shower? I'm all sweaty and someone spilled booze on me." He grimaced. "I reek of tequila."

Eric could only nod. "Guest bathroom is through there, down the hallway, first on the right. Spare guest towels in the cupboard under the sink."

Kyle winked, retrieved his bag and disappeared. Eric heard the bathroom door close and the shower start.

The door opened again and Kyle yelled, "You can get ready for me in your bedroom, if you like. I know we said we'd floor-fuck but I'm sure the bed will be much more comfortable on my arse. I'm not partial to rug burn." The door slammed shut again.

Eric needed no further prompting. He turned off the lights and took the two drinks into his bedroom. He placed one on each of the bed's side tables, switching on the bedside light and flooding the room with dim glow. Disrobing quickly, he folded his clothes into a neat pile on the dresser.

When he slid under the duvet, he turned to check he had lube and condoms stashed on the side table. Satisfied he did, he laid back, arms above his head and waited for Kyle.

The wait was worth every minute. Fifteen minutes later, Kyle appeared, fresh and naked, his cock half-mast along his smooth groin. He stopped in the doorway, framed by the light in the bedroom and grinned wickedly as he struck a seductive pose.

"Well," he drawled, watching Eric with hungry eyes. "If it isn't a hunk of paramedic in the bed, waiting to screw me senseless."

He prowled over to the bed, nipple rings glinting in the light. Eric wanted to tug on them with his teeth until he heard Kyle make a small sound of both desire and pain.

Kyle threw back the covers, and like a feral cat, he slinked up the bed to straddle Eric. The air left the room as he wriggled his arse against Eric's rising cock then smiled predatorily.

"Hello there," he purred.

Eric's thoughts jumbled in an already scrambled brain from Kyle's clean scent, the slide of his warm skin against him and the sheer wantonness he gave off as he leaned in to lick a slow trail around Eric's bottom lip.

This man is sex on a stick. I'm not sure I can handle him.

"Stop looking so damn worried," Kyle murmured. "I'm not going to eat you." The eyebrow with the ring in it rose suggestively. "Although that might be a lovely thing to do sometime."

He'd removed his purple contacts and his deep brown eyes shone with both humour and lust.

Eric could stand the teasing no longer. He reached out and pulled Kyle down to him. "I need to taste you."

The wet, open-mouthed kiss that followed sent his senses into further turmoil. From the sounds Kyle was making into his mouth, he was turned on too. His hardened cock pressed against Eric's abs, slicking their stomachs with arousal.

He was dimly aware of Kyle breaking the kiss and lying down beside him, legs akimbo, his desire evident as his hardened cock jutted into Eric's side.

"Enough of that," Kyle said breathlessly. "Time to fuck me."

Eric couldn't take his eyes off Kyle opening the lube bottle and pouring a liberal amount on his fingers. Then, like a sculptor caressing clay, Kyle reached between his legs and slid his finger around his hole, finally pressing inside.

His eyes closed, and his eyelashes fluttered as he fucked himself with his fingers. "Uhhm, yeah," he groaned. The next moan was louder.

Despite his arousal, Eric grinned when Kyle opened one eye, no doubt to gauge his reaction. *God, he's such a fucking tease.* "I think you've had enough fun, mister," he murmured as he slid over Kyle's sweat-sheened body. "It's my turn now. Move your damn hand. That's mine."

Eric caressed the outside of Kyle's rim then slid two fingers inside the warm, tight, wet hole. "This," he promised, and then he removed his fingers from Kyle arse. "And this," he groaned as he gripped Kyle's cock, sliding a clenched hand up and down.

Kyle uttered a strangled moan and Eric felt a surge of satisfaction as he watched those brown eyes grow glassy and unfocused while Kyle's breathing became uneven and deep.

"That feels so good," Kyle murmured breathily. "Imagine how it will feel when I have your beautiful cock inside me."

Eric leaned forward and tugged at the nipple ring with his teeth, causing Kyle's breaths to become erratic. "God, you are incredible," Eric whispered. "So damned responsive."

"Stop with the compliments and fuck me," was Kyle's strained response.

Eric chuckled as he rolled on the condom while Kyle watched avidly, lips wet, pupils flaring. Then, pushing Kyle's hands above his head, Eric held him down as he braced himself for entry into the sexiest creature he'd ever met.

When he breached Kyle's arse, both men gasped and froze, staring at each other.

Fuck, that feels good. He was made for me.

Sweat beaded on Kyle's face. "Stop being such a gentleman and keep going," he snarled, pushing his hips upward, impaling himself deeper. "I didn't say you could stop."

"You're such a bossy bastard," Eric grunted as he did what he was he told.

Then all conversation stopped. There was only the sensation of skin on skin, the taste of salt in his mouth from trickling sweat, and the slow and steady rush of blood in his veins making him feel more alive than he'd been in a long time.

Beneath him Kyle was pumping his hips, scratching sharp nails into Eric's back and uttering nonsensical panting moans as he gave himself over to his bliss.

The primal act of sex, of being as close to another human being as one could get, had always filled Eric with awe. With Kyle, though, he felt—god-like. Thrusting into the willing man writhing under him, feeling his pleasure like electric pulses beating through his cock—this was what it meant to be young and alive; to be part of something bigger than both of them.

And there was no doubt he wanted more of it.

"God," he gasped as his body prickled with heat and his balls contracted. "I'm not sure I can go any longer."

Kyle arched his neck, baring a slender, flushed throat. "Then blow, baby. Give me all you've got."

Eric exploded into the condom as his orgasm hit with avalanche-worthy force. He shuddered as the aftershocks hit, small tremors that shook his body and gave him goose bumps.

"Fuck, that was hot, seeing you come like that." In one fluid motion Kyle pushed Eric onto his back, and straddled him, his cock still inside Kyle. Eric was too spent to react other than look into the heated gaze of the man who currently held him captive in every way.

Kyle reached down and took hold of his own dick. "I want to shoot all over you, paint you like a masterpiece with my come." A few hard jerks resulted in exactly that. Hot, slick semen coated Eric's stomach and chest, and a few stray strands landed on his lips. He licked it away, relishing in the taste of Kyle in his mouth.

Kyle flopped down, boneless and sticky. For a moment neither one said anything then Eric ran a hand down the smooth flanks lying over him. "Epic as that was, we should clean up and get into bed." Eric closed his eyes, loathe to move but needing to breathe.

Kyle nodded, hair brushing Eric's nose and making him sneeze. "Sorry. Yeah, I guess we should do that." He moved off and flung his legs off the bed. "I'll go first." Kyle stood then disappeared into the bathroom.

Eric must have dozed off because when he opened his eyes, a warm body was snuggled up next to him. He rolled his shoulder against heated flesh; his arm had gone to sleep because Kyle was lying on it.

"Ugh," Kyle murmured. "That tickles." He shuffled a little further away and Eric stretched out his arm, trying to relieve the pins and needles.

"Don't worry," Kyle said sleepily as he snuggled a pert, warm arse in against Eric's front. "You were asleep when I came out so I cleaned you up and tucked you in. Go back to sleep."

Eric wrapped an arm around Kyle and drew him closer against him. "Thanks. Sorry I fell asleep."

"S'right," Kyle snuffled from the depths of the pillow. "Not the first time a bloke's gone to sleep afterwards."

Eric kissed the back of the fragranced hair that was still making his nose twitch. "I'm not surprised, if that's what sex with you is like. You really know how to take it out of a guy."

He felt a pang of jealousy for any other man who'd had Kyle this way.

Kyle's head shook fractionally and his muffled words filled Eric with hope. "Not like that with anyone else. Just you. Now go to fucking sleep, will you?"

Eric smiled widely and settled in. He could get used to this.

"No, you can't use a sex swing on the stage tonight. I've told you. The beams above are not strong enough to support you and your partner having bloody simulated sex."

Eric grinned as Kyle, looking more than frazzled, glowered at a two-hundred-pound drag queen who was battering her eyelashes shamelessly at his—boyfriend? He still wasn't quite sure what to call Kyle after the last two weeks. Two incredible weeks of hot sex, cuddles and finding out they both loved Vietnamese food. And Alexander Skarsgård.

They hadn't done much talking about personal stuff, but Eric was at the point where he felt he could talk about Lincoln. He only hoped Kyle would open up soon about whatever gave *him* nightmares.

Eric sighed. *We're a right pair; both of us with our bad dreams and three am wake-up calls. At least the cuddling each other back to sleep makes up for it.*

Cuddling that occasionally led to sleepy, comfort sex.

Tonight, it was the Annual Hoity Toity Tart Fashion Show at Club Delish. It was a major event and had driven Kyle to distraction, even with Ryan's limited help during the recovery stage of his convalescence.

Kyle paced up and down the stage, gesticulating angrily. "Calypso, I don't care what Delilah told you. Those beams won't hold you both and I have to think about health and safety." He glared at Calypso Cockbottom, who simply rolled her eyes at the dramatics.

"And it's not only you two I need to worry about," Kyle said cattily. "I have to worry about you both flattening anyone who might happen to be standing underneath you when the swing gives way."

Calypso opened her mouth and screeched in horror. "Oh, you little bitch. How dare you? It's not my fault you look like one of those candidates for Carnival of the Skinny Man Whore. Some of us love our extra pound of flesh. Don't we, Qunta?"

She flicked the Japanese fan she was holding in the direction of another queen, who stood on the side-lines, smirking at the show playing out centre stage. Eric had been highly entertained for the last ten minutes as the argument escalated, and had seen the amused glint in Calypso's eyes as she baited Kyle.

"Oh, yes, honey," Qunta Kryptonite agreed, as she simpered at her partner. "Some of us like a little something to hold onto while we fuck. We don't want to cut ourselves on the bones of said skinny man whore."

"I am not a man whore," Kyle said between gritted teeth. "And I'm not skinny. Am I, Eric?"

Shocked out of complacency, Eric thought quickly. "No, babe, you're not. Nice and lean is what you are." He sidled up to Kyle, lowering his voice. "You do know these two are just riling you up on purpose, don't you?"

Kyle looked at him and winked. "Oh yeah. It's a game we play. Hang on for the ride."

He strode over to Calypso and prodded her ample chest with each word he spoke. "You.Are.Not.Having.A.Sex.Swing.On.My.Stage. Got it?"

Calypso flapped her fan in his face and glared. "Fine. I'll talk to D. She'll let me have one." She flipped her long black hair over her shoulder and motioned to her partner. "Come on, darling. Let's go find Delilah. She won't be as bitchy as this one."

"Don't go busting her chops," Kyle warned. "She's still recovering from her surgery and you'll have Mango to deal with if you cause her grief."

They both looked worried for a moment. "We'll manage him," Calypso didn't look so sure, but waved a hand in Qunta's direction. "I'm sure two of us weighty bitches can handle little old Mango."

As the two queens exited stage-right, Calypso looked back and flipped her middle finger at Kyle. He flipped her back.

Eric shook his head. "Wow, this is something else. You need some sort of psych education and qualifications to deal with that kind of crazy."

Kyle sniggered. "I have it in spades. In Vegas, they were big, bold and brash, and you had to learn to give as good as you got. Calypso is pretty cool. She might go to Ryan and ask him and he'll tell her the same thing. He was the one who told me to stop the idea in its infancy. Not enough balls to do it himself." Kyle laughed loudly. "And Mango won't let them bug his man. He's become über-protective. That's why Ry hasn't been around much. Too busy being loved up and pampered by a reformed Mango. Mind you, Ry deserves it after all he's been through."

Kyle frowned and stuck out his hip with a turned wrist on it that angled his elbow at forty-five degrees. "So, you really think I'm not too skinny? I don't really care about the man whore comment because, well, there might be a grain of truth in that, but skinny? Pfffft."

Eric pulled Kyle's face toward him and planted a kiss on his lips. "No, you're just the right shape and size. We fit together perfectly."

Kyle smirked. "We do indeed. Like a mortar and pestle. Except my arsehole is tighter."

Eric couldn't help a guffaw at that. "Jeez, you have no filter."

Kyle sidled up and wrapped his arms around Eric's neck "And don't you love it. Thanks for changing your shifts around to help me here today. It's been a bonus." His lips found Eric's and he worked them into a deep and passionate kiss.

All thoughts of oversized drag queens dangling from sex swings disappeared from Eric's mind.

Chapter Eleven

Kyle peered around anxiously at the throng of people waiting to see the fashion show in support of Ryan's chosen charity—supporting brain tumour sufferers. Club Delish was full to brimming; the turnout had exceeded expectations.

"This is great," he muttered to Eric, who stood beside him. "Ryan is as high as a kite on the numbers."

Eric nodded. "I suspect it's *because* of Ryan. His customers hold him in high regard. I guess this is an opportunity for them to see he is well."

Kyle agreed. "It's his first proper public appearances on stage as Delilah Delish since the operation. And of course, Laverne is with him tonight." He laughed. "Those two together are always a hoot."

Ryan's best friend Lenny James a.k.a. Laverne was a well-loved character at Club Delish. It was her designs and those of her students that were being showcased tonight, with sales proceeds going to the charity.

Kyle sniggered. "I know Mango wasn't particularly thrilled that Ryan was performing 'only a month after he'd had fucking brain surgery.' The sight of Ryan giving the deadly laser gaze froze *my* blood, I can tell you. His response to Mango, 'Stop fucking molly coddling me and let me get back to being a normal man.' He's one scary dude."

Eric rolled his eyes.

"No, really. After the argument, they went upstairs and I'm betting there was a slap or two, and then no doubt sizzling make-up sex. That's the way that pair roll." Kyle sighed. "God, I hope everything goes well. I'm a nervous fucking wreck."

"Stop worrying." Eric massaged Kyle's shoulders. "It's all going to go off perfectly."

"You think?" Kyle nibbled on his nail. "There's been so much organisation, I can't help thinking I've forgotten something." *Maybe I didn't order enough booze, or toilet paper. Oh God, did I make sure the kegs were changed earlier?*

Eric chuckled. "Unless Calypso's installed that sex swing you told her not to, I can't see anything going wrong."

Kyle darted a swift glance to the rafters above to check nothing unwanted was swinging down.

Eric stifled a laugh. "Baby, you did good. Ryan even said so himself, didn't he?"

Kyle nodded distractedly. "I s'pose. He seemed pleased with all the arrangements, said he couldn't have done it better himself."

"There you go then. Relax."

"Easy for you to say," Kyle muttered, biting another fingernail.

Eric heaved a sigh and grasped Kyle's hand, moving it away from his mouth. "I can think of better things you can do with that mouth of yours other than bite your nails."

Kyle was about to reply when a female voice behind them startled him. "Hi, London. You look fabulous as usual. And this must be Eric." Kyle looked over to see Lucinda and her date.

Luce's eyes were speculative as she stared at Eric, and he hoped she wasn't going to go too crazy on his arse. This was the first time they were meeting, and Luce had already intimated she was going to grill him about his intentions. After everything she had been through extricating him from Mario's demented grasp, she was an overprotective mama bear.

He pushed that memory from his mind and smiled brightly. "Hey, gorgeous. I'm glad you made it. And who is this beautiful woman beside you?"

Luce laughed, eyes sparkling. "This is Lanie, my date. Lanie, my best pal, Kyle."

Lanie was tall, thin and blonde, and had an air of class Kyle suspected belonged only to the very rich. He presumed this was the Lanie with whom Luce had flown to Paris. Lanie had a charming smile and shook his hand warmly. "I've heard a lot about you from Lucinda. You two have shared some real fun experiences, huh, from your Vegas days?"

Panic shot through Kyle's chest and he flicked a worried glance at Luce. She shook her head slightly and instantly Kyle was relieved.

"I'm sure she's told you a lot of lies about me too." He bent over her hand and brushed his lips across her knuckles. "Don't judge. She's a continental bitch." He turned to pull his man forward. "This is Eric."

Lucinda inclined her head toward him. "Good to meet you at last, Eric. I've heard a lot about you."

Eric looked a little awkward. "Likewise. I'm really pleased to meet the woman who keeps him on the straight and narrow."

Kyle watched proudly as everyone shook hands. Eric looked sexy tonight in his black chinos, open dark blue shirt with just a hint of chest hair, and sleeves rolled up to his elbows, which put his strong forearms on display. Kyle had convinced Eric to use a little hair product tonight to tame his unruly curls, and he looked like a model about to walk down the catwalk.

Knowing Luce as he did, Kyle headed her off at the pass before the awkward Eric grilling began. "Well, you know where the bar is, Luce. I suggest you get you and your girl a drink and then sit down to watch the show. It's filling up quickly and I'd hate for you not to get a seat. I need to check on a few things." Kyle kissed Luce on her cheek then crocked a finger at Eric. "C'mon you. I need some help backstage to make sure all the queens are ready to start in fifteen minutes."

"Oh, is that what they're calling a quick shag in the back nowadays?" Luce said archly. "And not so fast, hotshot. I want to get to know Eric a little better first." She smiled like a Cheshire cat.

Kyle's heart sunk. That smile meant business.

"Eric, baby, what are your intentions towards my bestie? He's super special to me, and I want to make sure you treat him right." Beside her Lanie cast a sympathetic glance Kyle's way.

Eric crossed his arms across his chest and grinned at Lucinda. "My intentions? Wow, how much time do you have? Because my intentions are really detailed."

Kyle held back a chuckle. Luce looked taken aback, which was rare.

"I need to know you're not going to break his heart, and you're not in it just for the sex. Which I imagine is wild, given the looks of the two of you."

Kyle blushed scarlet. "Luce, for God's sake. I can look after myself. I don't need you being all mother hen on my arse. We've had this discussion before."

Eric drew him closer, putting a possessive arm around his waist. Kyle sank into the cuddle as his boyfriend's hand drifted down to stroke his arse.

"I can assure you, I have exceptionally good intentions toward Kyle, and he's special to me."

Kyle fluttered his eyelashes. "Aw gee. You gonna be my papa bear?"

Eric mock-growled, "If you like that sort of thing, boy, I'm not objecting. I have a leather harness with your name all over it."

They stared at each and then burst into laughter. Lucinda tossed her hair back but Kyle saw the pleased look on her face.

"Well, all righty then. Come on, Lanie. Let's get those mojitos we promised ourselves. Let these boys have their dirty fun 'helping each other backstage.'"

She pointed a finger at Eric. "But if anything happens to my friend, you'll have me to deal with as well."

She took Lanie's hand and dragged her through the milling crowd.

"She's a little scary," Eric confessed as they watched them go. "And I wouldn't want to face her in a dark alley."

"Yeah," Kyle said fondly. "She's great. We've been through a lot together."

"Maybe one day you'll tell me all about it," Eric murmured.

Kyle ignored that remark, took Eric's hand and drew him through the crowds toward the stage.

"So, is 'helping him backstage' a euphemism?" Eric asked.

"A euphemism for what?" Kyle was distracted by the sight of one of the patrons stripping off to reveal a nice six-pack.

"For us having raunchy sex." Eric flashed him a wicked grin.

Kyle wished it was. "Sorry to disappoint you, baby. It's an actual thing. Speaking to the raving drama queens in the back and making sure when the fashion show starts in"—he looked at his watch—"ten minutes, everyone is ready to go."

Good thing they'd checked. The queens were rebellious, disorganised and ornery. Kyle had to go on stage with a harried apology to the patrons that the show was running late. Finally, everything and everyone was sorted, and he and Eric were able to sit toward the back of the house, both with stiff drinks in their hands, while they watched as Delilah Delish swanned onto the stage.

Kyle's part was over. Now it was up to the performers and models on stage. He took a deep swig of his drink, leant back and closed his eyes in relief.

Eric nudged him. "She looks pretty good, doesn't she? I wish I could wear a white fringe dress and a black feather boa like she can."

Kyle stared at him. "Is that a secret fantasy of yours then? Dressing in drag?" He rather appreciated the idea. He could see that russet hair against a background of pale green headwear and Eric's long, muscled body squeezed into a—hmm, perhaps a dress like the one Alexander McQueen designed. Shades of deep red, bronze and white with a black feather trail.

Oh, yeah. Kyle's dick really liked that idea.

Eric raised an eyebrow. "Would it get you hot? Because I'll do anything that makes you want me."

Kyle leaned forward and ran a finger over Eric's lips. "You don't have to *do* anything to turn me on. You just do." He noted with satisfaction the darkening of Eric's green eyes and the unconscious lick of his lips. *Who's the man? You can still do it to him with just a few words.*

"Could my front of house manager please stop making out with his delicious man in plain sight and pay attention to what *I'm* saying?" The words from on stage echoed in the room. Startled, both looked up to see Delilah glaring at them from heavily made-up eyes. "There's time to suck his dick later."

Kyle snorted with laughter and Eric waved at Delilah who blew him a kiss.

"So, my darlings, you all know I've been a bit in the wars lately."

The room erupted in cheers and cries of "Welcome Back, D. We love you!"

Delilah acknowledged them with an incline of her perfectly coiffed wig. Only someone who knew her well would notice she was quite overcome with the support in the room. She cleared her throat, a sound that resounded into the microphone wired on her front.

"Of course, *someone* in this room"—she cast a withering stare at Mango who sat at the front of the stage—"was an overprotective papa bear and went all dom on my arse, not letting me do as much at the club as I'd have liked."

Mango stood up, a wide grin on his face, and gave a stately bow. He sat down, his gesture having everyone in fits of laughter, interspersed with ribald comments about what he was doing with Delilah's arse.

Sitting beside him was a tall, statuesque black man who said something to Mango. He burst into laughter. Kyle grinned. He'd met Brook Hunter, Laverne's boyfriend, only a few times and had really enjoyed his company.

"In my considerable absence"—an icy stare was once again thrown Mango's way—"my right-hand man, Kyle Tripper, has been running our club."

Kyle noticed the slight emphasis on "our" and his body flushed with warmth at the acknowledgment of his part. Eric squeezed Kyle's hand and looked at him with affection.

"He is my greatest asset, other than these." Delilah cupped her breasts to the support of laughter and jeers. "And I'm fortunate to have him. I'd like to say a huge thank you, my love, for organising tonight and making it such a success, despite the whinges from the bitches backstage. I think we owe this young man a round of applause. He already has my eternal thanks for keeping Club Delish going while I was otherwise indisposed."

Kyle's face heated up as everyone clapped and hooted, and Mango nodded thanks and gave him a thumbs-up.

When the merriment was over, Delilah turned to face the stage wings. She curtsied and as she did so, another queen made her entrance.

Laverne was clad in a slinky black ensemble with grey sleeves resembling bat wings. She glided in on ten-inch heels and the audience erupted into catcalls.

Delilah sported a wide grin as the two women air-kissed, the sound of smacking lips exaggerated before Delilah said, "The delightful Laverne and her assistant Leslie Scott will now announce her designs and the next models. I wish you a wonderful night right through until the end of the show. I'll be back soon, sweethearts. I promise. Just got a little rough and tumble to go take care of." She made a lewd and lascivious gesture to Mango who shook his head in amusement.

Laverne took centre stage. Kyle perked up when a figure he knew quite well swished in next to Laverne. Willowy and black haired, Leslie Scott was the epitome of style in a hand-cut lilac suit crossed with a dove-grey shirt and a darker grey waistcoat. He was a delicious sight to behold, although Kyle knew Leslie's boyfriend, Oliver, would have his guts for garters if he'd ever made a move on him. Besides, he had his own man now.

"Bitches," Laverne shrieked as she surveyed the crowd. "Let's get the party started. The gorgeous Leslie here is going to accompany the models on their way down the catwalk and add a little bit of glam to the proceedings. Because they sure as fuck need it with the bunch of queens we've got down here." She smirked and batted her long eyelashes at the audience.

"Looks like the models are ready for us. First up in an ensemble of violet taffeta and silk bronze trim, designed by me of course, world-famous fashion icon, Laverne Debussy-Smith. And here is the oh-so-edible and charming Calypso Cockbottom."

Laverne flourished a hand toward the woman currently mincing onto the stage as she resumed speaking. Leslie walked over to Calypso, holding out his elbow.

"All these dresses are available to purchase at extremely affordable prices, with all the proceeds going to Club Delish's chosen charity, Going Grey, which supports the work being done on research into brain tumours. Buy a dress for you, your wife, your mistress, your boy, your boyfriend, your favourite drag queen…we thank you for any support you can give us."

Eric laughed beside Kyle. "My God, this place is a hoot tonight. I'm loving all the cattiness."

A voice shouted Kyle's name, and he turned to see his new friend Louis, who looked resplendent in a charcoal grey suit, wine silk shirt and a white and burgundy spotted tie.

Despite being happy to see Louis, Kyle was also a little apprehensive. He hadn't told Eric about his new friend yet. *I hope they get on with each other. Louis can be a bit—intense.*

Kyle stood up to greet Louis, and as he did, he was pulled into a hug and a smacking kiss was planted onto his cheek.

"Hello there, my gorgeous man. This place looks amazing. Those queens look fantastic in those outfits. I may have to invest in one. Perhaps I will wear it out next time we go to dinner." Kyle was enveloped in another hug fragranced with Paco Rabanne and the faint smell of cigars.

"Hi, Louis. It's good to see you too. You're looking as handsome as usual."

Louis finally let him go and Kyle looked over at Eric, whose face was filled with what looked like astonishment and, he hoped, perhaps a tinge of jealousy.

He hastened to introduce the two men. "Louis, I need you to meet Eric. Eric, this is my friend Louis. We met while you were away."

Louis held out a hand to Eric, who took it. "So, you are the man he talks nonstop about. It's a pleasure to meet you." He stepped back and waved a hand toward Kyle. "At the time we met, I was trying to talk him into having a drink with me with an intention to perhaps enjoy a little more of his company. He politely declined. I can see why now. You look enticing in that ensemble. I had no idea black chinos and a grey wool blazer could look so alluring on a man. And I love the black oxfords. Very chic." He grinned, showing white teeth. Kyle stifled a chuckle at the dumbfounded expression on Eric's face, not having been able to get a word in edgeways.

"Babe, Louis will grow on you. He tends to have no filter so he spews stuff out at an alarming rate without even knowing he's doing it. And you know what, I don't think I told you how hot you look tonight. Because you do look sexy as fuck."

Eric blinked and then slowly nodded. "Yeah, thanks, to both of you. So, you two have been seeing each other then?" His gaze landed on Kyle. "You hadn't mentioned it before."

Kyle shrugged. "What with everything going on, it slipped my mind." He turned to Louis. "I reserved you a seat down the front. It has your name on it. Grab yourself a drink and enjoy the rest of the show. I'll catch up with you later."

Louis reached over to hug Kyle again. "Indeed, we will. Do not leave without saying goodbye."

Kyle and Eric watched Louis plunge his way through the crowd. Kyle sat down and reached over to take Eric's hand. "So, what do you think? He's great, isn't he?"

Eric shifted uncomfortably. "I don't know him well enough yet. If you like him, then I guess he must be. He's a bit—handsy, isn't he?"

Kyle made a sound suspiciously like a man giggle and then clapped a hand over his mouth. That sound surely hadn't come out of his mouth, had it?

His man was jealous. Kyle wanted to milk this just a little more.

"Oh, he's a bit affectionate. It's just how he is. Does it bother you?"

Eric looked a little affronted. "I wouldn't ever tell you who can and can't touch you, babe. That's your decision." He leaned in and brushed Kyle's cheek tenderly. "I just don't want him thinking he can ever take you away from me. Because I'm not letting you go without a fight." He smiled softly.

Kyle's eyes filled unexpectedly as the words sunk in. His heart beat erratically and he thought he might explode from the feels.

Eric really wanted him. He would fight for him. And he might be jealous, but he accepted Kyle's responsibility for his own body and his own wellbeing.

He wasn't Mario.

"Wow, that's pretty deep." He tried to make light of it, but his throat was a little choked. "Lucky then I'm not thinking of going anywhere, huh?"

Eric pulled Kyle's chair flush with his, and for a while they were both oblivious to the sounds around them as their kiss became the only thing that mattered.

It was close to two am when an exhausted Kyle was shooed away from the club by an equally exhausted Ryan.

"Go home," he instructed, blue eyes tired yet the look on his face was one of satisfaction. The amount of money raised for the evening had far exceeded expectations. "Rufus is doing the final checks to see we don't have unexpected overnight visitors, and Greg, bless him, is going to close up for me."

Ryan looked as if he couldn't keep his eyes open, and as Mango strode toward him, Kyle had no doubt Ry would be rushed to bed and tucked in before the door was even locked.

Mango's face showed his concerned. "Babe, you've overdone it, as usual. Come on. Let me get you upstairs. I'll carry you if you like." He grinned. "I've done it before, remember?"

Ryan flapped a hand and scowled. "You big ape, I'm not a damsel in distress. I can make it on my own, don't *you* remember?" His tone was fond and the loving glance he gave his boyfriend made Kyle wonder if he might find the same thing with Eric. "Now, shoo, you two. And Kyle, baby?" Ryan reached over and pulled Kyle into a fierce hug. "Thank you. For tonight and every other night. I couldn't have managed to get through all this without you there looking after this place."

Kyle's throat clogged up with emotion and he hugged Ryan back. "No problems, boss. Glad to help anytime. You get to bed, and sweet dreams."

Mango gave him a quick, awkward pat on the back. "Yeah, what he said. Ry's been lucky to have you in his corner. Appreciate you looking out for him."

Kyle spotted Eric on the other side of the room, helping Greg pick up overturned chairs in the private area and setting them right. Eric waved, his smile lighting up his features.

Kyle waved back, and Ryan laughed. "Go on, fuck off you two. Go do the horizontal mamba if you can manage it. Me, I don't think I can even manage to stay awake long enough to enjoy a blowjob." The sly look he gave Mango made Kyle doubt that was true.

He chuckled. "Great. See you Monday." He walked over to Eric who beamed at him. "Ready to go? I'm about to drop where I stand."

Eric's face brightened. "What, right here? Isn't that a bit public?"

Kyle punched Eric on the arm. "Is that all you think about—sex?" He collected his jacket from the back of the reception desk and handed Eric his. "Come on. Let's go home."

Home tonight was Kyle's place. They decided to walk, shift off some cobwebs and the scent of being stuck in the sweaty and testosterone-reeking club all night.

The evening air was chill, the streets still vibrant with people. Eric offered his elbow to Kyle who took it, a warm feeling in his chest that he wasn't averse to displaying affection in public. Kyle wouldn't go further—he'd learnt his lesson about unwanted PDAs the hard way, so kissing or making out in public was a no-no—but the snug feel of his arm tucked into Eric's was soothing. He felt safe and cherished.

The dream was shattered when a sudden push at his back caused him to stumble, twisting to fall awkwardly on the pavement. Instinctively, he put his arms up to shield his body and face. Before he blocked out the view, he caught a glimpse of a familiar figure. A tall, dark-haired man loomed toward him, something swinging from his right arm.

Fuck, he's found me.

Beside him Eric shouted something, but Kyle couldn't hear. His ears were buzzing, bile had collected in the back of his throat and overwhelming fear claimed his body and mind like an invasive entity that drove all rational thought from his brain and made him remember all the abuse he'd suffered.

The words that came out of his mouth were strangled and fearful, ones he thought he'd never utter again. "Mario, I'm sorry. Please don't...."

Something wet hit his face, unwanted and foul smelling. Kyle curled into a ball, waiting for the kicking to start. Instead, strong arms encircled him in their warmth, and dimly he recognised the scent of Eric's aftershave.

"Babe, he's gone. It was just a guy on the lam. I think he snatched a handbag. He ran into you. Are you okay? Are you hurt?"

Kyle shuddered and moved his arms away from his face. Anxious green eyes stared into his, as fingers gently wiped something from his face.

"He spat at you. I want to clean you up. I don't want anything of that bastard's on you. Can you stand? Come on. Hold onto me. We're not far from your flat. Let's get you home."

Eric helped Kyle stand. His body shook but it wasn't from fear alone. He felt ashamed and embarrassed, and was sure Eric would leave him now—because who'd want a man like him?

So indelible, his self-loathing mixed with the current panic, creating a miasma of dark emotions he thought would destroy him.

He let Eric guide him along the busy street, and when they reached his block of flats, it was Eric who led Kyle into the grumbling lift and to the front door of his home. It was Eric who reached into Kyle's pocket and drew out the keys to unlock the door.

But it was Kyle who turned to Eric when they were safely inside, the door shut and locked, and quietly said, "Thank you for seeing me home. I appreciate it. You don't have to stay with me. You can leave. I'd understand if you don't want to come back." Of course he would mind. He'd scream and cry at his own failure until he was drained and comatose.

Eric stared at him, face grim, eyes haunted. "I'm not leaving until I know you're okay. And why the fuck wouldn't I want to come back?"

The bedroom seemed like the right place to be right now, buried under the covers, so Kyle moved toward it, not answering. *I just want to sleep and forget all this for a while. Maybe it'll take this ache in my chest away.*

"Kyle? Talk to me. Please." Eric sounded wounded. He sighed sadly and turned to face Kyle, who had trouble meeting Eric's gaze.

"You must think I'm pathetic. How can you not? I see a person that looks like someone from my past and I fall to pieces. What kind of man does that make me?" Eyes stinging, he walked toward his room. "I won't think any less of you if you don't want to see me anymore."

"Kyle." Eric's tone was fierce. "I'm having trouble with all this."

He laughed harshly. "That's why I said you could leave."

"No." Eric appeared at his side but he made no attempt to touch him. "I meant I'm having trouble with you thinking I'm the sort of man who'd kick you to the kerb because you have some sort of PTSD. I thought you knew me better. I'm disappointed you would even consider I'd do something shitty like that." He didn't wait for an answer. He strode over to Kyle and gathered him into his arms. "I'm not going anywhere. Get used to it. Because you and I—we need to seriously talk about things."

Kyle stopped and let the fatigue wash over him like a veil. Hope flickered in his chest like a small candle. "Are you sure? I mean—"

Soft lips pressed against his and then lingered over his cheek. "I'm sure. You and I—we're the same. I know exactly what you're going through because I've been through it myself. But this isn't about me right now. All I want you to know is that I understand. And I'm not leaving."

Kyle let himself collapse against Eric's broad chest as tears fell while he surrendered to Eric's embrace. Before he knew it, he was undressed, bundled into bed and a duvet was drawn across his body.

"Sleep now. We'll talk in the morning." Eric kissed Kyle's forehead then brushed a strand of hair from his face. "I'm going to take the couch so I don't disturb you. I'll be around if you need me. I'll leave some clean clothes on the dresser for you."

"'Kay," Kyle muttered, his body warm and languid under the covers. "Thanks, baby. For everything."

The light went out and he fell into sleepy darkness.

Tick. Tick. Tick.

Kyle watched the second hand move around the clock at the side of his bed and groaned softly. He'd been lying awake now for over an hour, summoning up the courage to get up. He thought he might be smiling like an idiot.

He's still here.

He heard Eric moving around the kitchen and smelt coffee brewing, which was scented heaven. That alone should have him scrambling out of bed ready to face the day. But he needed another few minutes to gather his thoughts and plan what he was going to say when he faced Eric.

The sharp rap on the door made him jump.

"Hi, sleepy-bones. Get your lazy arse out of bed and come get your coffee. I know you're awake. I heard you sighing like a woman out of some Victorian melodrama."

Kyle bolted upright indignantly. "I so did not. I was thinking."

There was a muffled, amused snort outside the door. "Yeah, well, stop thinking and come have some breakfast. I'm making your favourite."

"You made me French toast?" Kyle swung his legs over the bed, a smile forming.

There was silence. "Oh, French toast is your favourite? I thought it was eggs over easy on rye bread." Eric sounded a bit put out and

Kyle chuckled, feeling better. "Anyway, you've got a few minutes to shower—the eggs are going now."

Kyle showered in record time, slung on some sweatpants and a tee-shirt and left his room feeling decidedly better than when he'd gone in the night before. He found Eric in nothing but jeans, his chest bare, dishing out eggs onto already buttered toast.

God, he looks good enough to eat.

"This, ermm, all looks good." Kyle waved at the small two-person dining table. The coffee pot was on the table, the mugs already filled. It was the picture of domesticity.

Eric grinned. "I hope you don't mind me taking over your kitchen. I promise I'll clean up, Mr Neat Freak."

Kyle noticed with dismay how untidy his usually pristine kitchen was. Eggshells lurked in plain sight. Crumbs were scattered across every surface and there was even a piece of burnt toast casually flung on top of the tea towel. Fat spattered up the white backsplash tiles. He swallowed, trying not to let the state of his kitchen affect him too much. "No problem. I see you're one of those chefs who really get into what they're doing."

Eric cocked his head to one side as he slid Kyle's plate over to him. "Is that your way of telling me I'm a messy bastard in the kitchen? Because I know I am. I mess first, clean later."

He sat down with his plate and took a slurp of coffee. "God, that's what I needed. Now eat, before it gets cold."

The food was tasty and Kyle hadn't realised how hungry he was. When they'd finished eating, he managed to convince Eric to leave the cleaning up. Kyle found it therapeutic; plus, it meant he could get things cleared the way *he* wanted them. It also delayed their conversation, which he wished there was a way to avoid altogether.

When he'd finished, he went to the lounge to join Eric, who was lying on the couch, legs stretched out. Kyle sat down in the armchair and looked across at him. "That was great, thanks. It's been ages since anyone did that for me."

Eric raised an eyebrow. "Good, I'm glad you enjoyed it. And don't think I didn't notice your attempt at getting me out of your kitchen so you could clean up your way. I would have cleared my own mess."

Kyle nodded. "I know. It's just I like things done a certain way, so…" He fiddled with the drawstring of his sweatpants.

The room went silent.

"Are you going to tell me what happened last night?" Eric shifted on the couch, turning on his side. When Kyle didn't answer, he went straight for the jugular. "Who is Mario?"

Kyle cleared his throat then exhaled. "He was my ex in Vegas. We were together around five months."

Eric's eyes narrowed. "He was abusive?"

Kyle nodded. "You could say that." His fingers clenched together.

What the fuck am I saying? The guy nearly killed me.

He closed his eyes, carefully choosing his next words. He sensed Eric's presence on the arm of the chair before he opened his eyes.

Eric ran a comforting hand down his back. "You going to tell me more? I don't want to push too hard."

Kyle took a deep breath, and then, like a floodgate had opened, it all came out. Torrents of fear, shame and pain mixed in with the need to tell this man next to him, this decent man, exactly why he'd acted like a scared child last night.

"Mario was older than me. He was a backup dancer at the casino. We met during one of the stage shows when I went backstage to deliver some drinks. I worked bar for extra money when I wasn't on the tables."

The memory of the night he'd first seen Mario flooded back. The dressing room had been empty apart from a few men busy disrobing and wiping makeup off their faces. He'd noticed Mario straight away, having seen him perform, and had been smitten.

Mario was dark, tall and muscled, with a dancer's grace. He'd smiled at Kyle when he'd taken his drink, and before Kyle had known it, he'd given Mario his number and arranged to meet him the following day after the show. That had been the start of Kyle's nightmare.

Eric moved over to the couch and patted the seat beside him. "We'll be more comfortable over here," he muttered softly.

Kyle moved to sit next to Eric and leaned in to Eric's side. The contact gave him strength to tell his story.

"Mario was Italian, and Catholic—staunchly so. He was bisexual, but nobody knew. If his family had found out, they'd have disowned him. They were deeply religious. Him having a nice boy slut on the side was all he wanted."

Eric said nothing, but made soothing circles on Kyle's back.

"I thought I was in love with him. He was charismatic, great in bed and spoilt me like crazy. I thought we were a great couple. Then suddenly, everything changed."

He slid closer to Eric. "His uncle Roberto from Italy came to live with the family. He was a priest who was cold and uncompromising. Mario adored him. He began spending time with him, and less with me. At first, I thought it was a family duty thing. Family meant everything to him." Kyle's throat grew tight. "One night he came over to my place in a foul mood after spending the day with his uncle. Roberto must have said something to him, because Mario stormed into my bedroom and…" The memory of that first assault came flooding back. "He hit me. With his fists, again and again, sending me halfway across the room."

Oh God, I can't tell him the rest of it. I can't.

Eric's hands stopped and he moved back, his face a masque of fury. "No reason? He just came in and beat the shit out of you?"

Kyle nodded jerkily. "The scariest thing—he didn't say a word. There was just this disgusted look on his face, as if I were a piece of shit. Then he left the room. I managed to get to the bathroom and clean up, but I was pretty out of it. I went back to bed and must have fallen asleep. When I woke up, he was there beside me, cleaning my face and putting ointment on it. He said he was sorry, that he'd never do it again."

Kyle closed his eyes and heaved a juddering sigh. "And I believed him. For a while, we were okay, went back to normal. That was when I met Luce at the club. She came to my rescue one night when he was getting mouthy. Told him to piss off and find someone his own size to pick on." He smiled at a better memory this time, one of meeting a crazy woman with pink hair telling his boyfriend exactly what she thought of him.

Of course, he'd never told her that had led to a beating when he got home. Luce would never have forgiven herself. It had been worth that beating to hear someone stand up to Mario like Kyle never had.

"Did you tell her about Mario beating you?" Eric's face was stony.

"No, not then. Things seemed all right, so I thought…no need for anyone else to get involved. Until it happened again. And kept happening. It was as if Mario was a different person. An evil, sadistic bastard, whose only intent was to hurt me. He said I brought out the 'dark touches' in him." Kyle laughed cynically. "Apparently what we did sexually was all my fault."

Kyle looked at the floor. "It's why that time we first went out I got spooked when you asked me about a lip ring. I used to have one, and a tongue stud, but the bastard tried to rip them out with his teeth a couple of times." He stroked his upper lip. "You can still see a faint scar if you look really closely."

He cleared his throat and continued, "Finally, I had to tell Luce about the fucked-up relationship I'd had with Mario. I had too many bruises and she was observant. Hell, she was so pissed off I had to stop her going to the cops. She had no idea what Mario was like. He wouldn't have gone quietly, and I didn't want her getting hurt." He grimaced. "As it happened, it wasn't long after that it all came to a head anyway."

Eric blew out a puff of air. "Didn't you have anywhere else to go? What kept you there?"

Kyle stared at him. "What kept me there was his threat to harm Luce if I left him, or went to the police. He threatened to beat her face in if I didn't stay with him. And he would have done it too. I had no doubt. He hated her, was jealous of the time we spent together. I tried to explain we worked together, so we had to see a lot of each other, but he didn't like it. I could have gone back to my parents in Chicago, but then what would have happened to Luce? Her life was there at that club."

"You stayed to keep her safe."

"Not just for that, but mainly. I thought I loved the man. Each time he beat me, I forgave him. I was stupid. His uncle was telling him about the sins of homosexuality, and it was driving him crazy. Mario needed the sex, the kink, but he thought it was a sin. He took it out on me, the so-called 'instrument' of his failing with God. If I even uttered a swear word which he thought was blasphemous, it led to another beating. I was in over my head. I didn't know what to do."

Eric squinted, "What kink?"

"Huh?"

"You said he had a kink. What was it?"

Kyle's bones chilled. "Oh, nothing, it was just an expression."

"Kyle." Eric's tone was compassionate. "Speaking from experience, if you're to have any hope of dealing with your PTSD, you're going to have to face the demon who put it there."

"Why don't you tell me *your* story?" Kyle spat, trying desperately to head Eric off. "You said you've got experience—well, tell me about it."

Eric's face clouded over with pain and Kyle felt like a heel for causing it. "I promise I will. But first, you need to finish yours."

The shame of Kyle's past washed over him. "Rough sex, okay? Mario liked rough sex when he went all Avenging Angel on my arse. He used to beat me, bloody me up then fuck me—no condoms, no lube, just straight. He said it would teach me a lesson and I deserved to be hurt for what I did to tempt him into sinning. The last time he did it, I suffered a ruptured rectum and had to be rushed to hospital. He'd hurt me so badly, I was in there over a week. They said I could have died. If Luce hadn't found me, I would have." Kyle was hyperventilating now, his hands shaking and body trembling.

"I'm sorry, baby, so sorry. I shouldn't have pushed you. Forgive me." Eric's whispered anguished words were heartfelt and Kyle tucked himself into Eric's chest, listening to the heartbeat under his ear.

"It's okay," Kyle murmured as tears slid down his cheeks, their saltiness lingering on his lips. "I feel better for having told you." He brushed Eric's jawline with his fingertips. He did feel better letting that out.

Finally, Eric looked up, eyes shining. "God, what you went through. I can't believe it. I hope that bastard got locked up for everything he did to you. If he didn't, I'll hunt him down and fucking kill him." The violence in Eric's tones was scary, and something Kyle hadn't heard from him before. A frisson of fear breathed cold air down his spine.

Eric would never hurt me. He saves lives; he doesn't damage them.

"Unfortunately, no. After the ambulance took me away, he rushed home to his uncle. I assumed he told him what he'd done because when I told the police about it, they went to his house and were told he'd gone away. I think his uncle spirited him back to Italy. The cops looked for him, but he'd gone to ground. Luce said there was a rumour he'd gone to a seminary in Europe somewhere to become a priest, but that was unverified."

"Did the police contact Interpol? He almost killed you, for God's sake." Eric hugged Kyle tighter.

"They did, but I think they gave up when there were no sightings of Mario anywhere. You know how it is. Something else more important comes up than a gay man being beaten by his lover." Kyle leaned into his boyfriend's comforting embrace. "The last time I heard from him was a crazy telephone call telling me how I'd messed up his life, that God may never forgive him, and that he was going to hunt me down and make sure I never did it to anyone else."

"Did the cops take the threat seriously?" Eric asked between clenched teeth.

Kyle nodded. "I think it's over, but seeing someone who looks or acts like him still triggers the trauma all over again." The telling had been cathartic and he was exhausted. "Now you know it all. I'm sorry I ended up a whimpering mess last night." He picked at his fingernails. "Luce has been telling me to see someone about it. A therapist. Maybe I will." He had the number of someone she'd recommended. He thought perhaps now was a time to call him.

"I think that's good advice." Eric shifted away and stood. "I feel like I've been through an emotional wringer, so I can imagine how you feel. What say I go make some cocoa, then we can sit on the couch, watch a film and snuggle under the duvet for a while? That work for you?"

Kyle smiled weakly. "That sounds fabulous." He hesitated. "Don't forget you owe me some details too. Maybe when we're in a better place, you can tell me. I think we've both had enough angst for one day."

Eric nodded. "Why don't you get the duvet? I'll get the drinks."

Kyle leaned back and closed his eyes, curling in the safe warmth of the spot Eric had just vacated.

Yawning, Kyle stretched and untangled himself from the duvet. Peering outside, he saw London enveloped in drizzle and mist. Dim shapes of people huddled under umbrellas were reminiscent of a painting by Rauf Janibekov, one of his favourite artists.

There was a sudden crash in the street and he jumped. Walking over to the window, he saw two people in the road gesticulating wildly as they each surveyed the damage to their cars. People passed by in the torrential rain, seemingly oblivious to the heated discussion of insurance culpability.

He shook his head and walked over to the kitchen. He found Eric in there, peering out into the road, coffee mug in hand. He turned when he heard Kyle come in. "Hi, sleepyhead." He gestured outside. "Silly buggers playing bumper cars out in this weather. I was checking to see they were okay, but they look unharmed. I hope you don't mind me taking over your kitchen but I needed coffee."

"As long as there's enough left for me." Kyle ran a hand over his bare chest, catching a glimpse of himself in the cupboard glass. He winced. His tousled hair stuck up like porcupine spikes and he had dark circles under his eyes. He hitched up his sweatpants.

Eric nodded and took down a fresh mug to fill it with strong black coffee. "I always make loads of extra coffee," he said as he handed the mug over. "It's the only thing that keeps me on time for my shifts most days."

Kyle took the mug gratefully and padded to the couch. He sat down to look out the window at the rain.

Eric plonked down beside him. "Did you have a good nap? You looked so relaxed. I didn't have the heart to wake you. You must have been exhausted."

Kyle nodded. "I was, a bit," he confessed. "Baring your soul takes it out of you." He hesitated. "Thanks for being there for me earlier. I'm not used to telling people that story. I know I'm a weakling who should have had the balls to stand up to a bully, but that's easier than it sounds."

Eric reached over and took Kyle's hands in his, rubbing them gently. "You have nothing to apologise for. And I get it—truly, I do. I see people every day in bad situations just like the one you were in and you can't judge them. No one knows what's going on in their heads. All you can do is lend support and try and get them to take care of themselves."

He scowled. "And you're no weakling. You re-made your life, and not everyone can say that about themselves."

Kyle gave a happy sigh, feeling safe and warm as he snuggled into Eric's chest and placed a kiss against his throat. "Thank you. That means a lot to me."

They sat together, Kyle listening to the beat of Eric's heart. "What are your plans for the rest of today?"

Eric hugged him closer. "It's raining out, as you can see, so indoors sounds like a good call. Maybe you can show me some more of those tricky card games. Teach me a couple, maybe?"

Kyle grinned, feeling more relaxed. "I'm sure I have a few up my sleeve you could learn."

"Then cards it is." Eric went to the dresser and pulled out an old deck of cards. "Show me how you did it in Vegas, baby."

Chapter Twelve

"Hell's bells," Eric muttered to Aaron in disgust. "Look at those fucking people. Like hyenas." He scowled at them fiercely. These last three days had been a bitch, so why should today be any different? The crowd around them had phones out, taking pictures of their latest incident and Eric wanted to swear at them, run over and yank the gadgets out of their hands.

They'd taken a call out for a woman who'd collapsed during the busy Saturday morning rush hour. After fighting their way through traffic and cursing at cars blocking their way, Eric and Aaron had finally arrived at the scene.

It took all of Eric's skills to move the man hovering over the woman's supine body away to let Aaron look at her. His partner's eyes conveyed the result to him even before he'd spoken the words. Aaron stood up and faced the middle-aged man in front of him.

"Sir, what's your name?" he asked gently.

"Jeremy. Jeremy Woden. My wife's name is Emily."

The man clenched his hands together as he gazed down at his stricken wife. "Emily, Emily, wake up," he sobbed, reaching down and pulling at her lifeless body. "The ambulance is here, you have to wake up."

Aaron's face was grave with sadness. "Jeremy, I'm so sorry to tell you this. Emily is gone. I think she might have been dead a little while. How long were you trying to wake her up?"

"Emily isn't gone," Jeremy spat out, tears rolling down gaunt cheeks. "She can't be. I've been talking to her for the last fifteen minutes."

Aaron threw a look of compassion at the man. "My gut feeling is she's had an aneurysm. It would have been quick. What do you mean, you talked to her for fifteen minutes? Did she respond at all?"

Jeremy's face clouded. "No, she didn't answer, but I swear I saw her eyes move. I thought if I talked to her, she'd wake up."

Eric stifled a weary sigh. The chances were that they wouldn't have been able to do anything if it had been an aneurysm, but waiting that long to call an ambulance had certainly lessened the woman's chances.

"Who called you anyway?" Jeremy asked wildly. "I didn't ask for anyone to come. I was going to wake her up and take her home."

A voice called out from the crowd. A slim Asian woman waved at them. "I did. I thought she needed an ambulance." Eric walked over to her. She was one of the few that didn't have a phone in her hand, merely a concerned expression on her face.

"Thank you," he said softly. "I think it's too late but you did what you could."

"Oh my God." The petite woman's face paled and her eyes filled with tears. "How tragic. That poor man."

The screech of absolute pain and grief from behind him made Eric's skin crawl, and goose bumps crept over his body. He turned around just in time to see Jeremy Woden run like a scared rabbit toward the entrance to the parking garage. His face was white but determined, and instinct made Eric run after him.

"Jeremy, stop, let's talk," he shouted as he followed the man up the winding turns of the driveways. Jeremy seemed intent on getting as high as he could. Eric had a bad feeling about this.

The sudden constriction in his chest had little to do with the fact he was exerting himself—he was fit—and more to do with the onset of something that felt very much like a panic attack.

If Jeremy was going to do what Eric thought he was going to, he wasn't sure he could deal with it.

I have to stop him.

Jeremy must have been a runner because he sprinted away fast, leaving Eric behind. The next thing Eric knew as he reached the fourth floor level was that he was too late. Jeremy was perched on the ledge, crouched low, muttering words Eric couldn't hear. He swallowed as he moved toward the determined man. "Jeremy, please calm down. I just need you not to move, 'kay?"

Jeremy stared back at him with dulled eyes. "It's all right," he reassured Eric, his face relaxing. "I know what I'm doing." He shrugged. "I can't live without her, don't you see? It's not something I can do."

He smiled at Eric and peace had suffused his face. "Thank you for trying to help anyway."

Eric could see the decision in his eyes. He'd seen it before. Adrenaline, shock, whatever it was, it propelled him forward to grab at Jeremy's arm. Before Eric could do anything more, the ledge was empty and all he held was the pale blue cardigan Jeremy had been wearing.

"No," he screamed as he dashed forward and looked over the side. He'd never forget the sight of the broken body lying four floors down, Aaron running toward it. It bore no resemblance to the man who only a few seconds ago had been on the ledge.

Bile rose in his throat as his chest tightened. He retched over and over again. Memories of another time and another man lying broken among rock and dust blinded him and pressed shards of sharp glass into his heart.

"Fuck," he coughed up as yellow fluid splashed onto the concrete floor. "Why did he jump?"

He dropped to his knees, uncaring of the fact he'd just coated his trousers with his own vomit as he knelt. The light around him grew dimmer; it was harder to breathe. He was dimly aware of a strong arm pulling him to his feet and forcing bottled water down his throat.

He barely registered the walk to the ambulance, supported by Aaron who murmured words of comfort in his ear. It was only when he was in the passenger side of the truck, eyes wet, chest heaving with sobs, that he realised he still held the cardigan in his hands.

Later that night, stretched out on the couch, Eric couldn't relax. Memories of the day played in his brain in a permanent loop. Aaron had gotten him back to the station and explained to their boss what had happened—panic attack, yes, like PTSD, past loss, needs a bit of time—while Eric looked on, feeling ashamed.

His protests had held no weight with either Aaron or their boss, Jim, and now Eric found he had an unscheduled couple of days off.

Taken home like a fucking damsel in distress, he thought grumpily as he tried to get comfortable. What a clusterfuck.

His mobile chirped and he glanced at it and sighed.

Kyle.

He forced a note of normality into his voice. He simply wasn't ready to talk about the day yet. "Hey," he said, plumping up a cushion with his free hand and leaning back on it. "Everything all right?"

He and Kyle had only managed to see each other once in the past few days, work pressures being as they were. It had seemed strange being apart so long after their last intimate conversation when Kyle had revealed all.

"Yeah, all good. I was wondering if you were in the mood for company?" Kyle's tone was hopeful. "For some reason, Ryan seems intent on helping me with my love life and giving me more time off. I'm not complaining. He has someone else starting next week as a trainee manager. Her name's Kellie. She's a fun lady. I'm hopeful she'll do well and we'll both get some more time off."

"That sounds so like Ryan. He's a good man." Eric picked a thread off the couch. "How can she not be a good fit if you like her?"

I really want to see him, but I'm in no mood for company tonight, not even Kyle. He doesn't deserve my shit. He's been through enough.

"Mmm, flattery gets you everywhere." Kyle sounded as if he was smiling. "So, you up for it? Me popping round? I'll even bring pizza. You owe me a conversation too. Fair's fair."

Eric chose his words carefully. There was no way he was telling Kyle about anything from his past tonight. Maybe not ever, on second thought. "Um, do you mind if I take a rain check? I've had a shitty day, and I'm awful company."

There was silence.

Then Kyle spoke brightly. "Oh, okay. You need some time to yourself. I get it. No worries. Have a good night and let me know when you're feeling better. See you."

The phone went dead.

Eric slapped a hand against his forehead. Crap, had he just pissed Kyle off or not?

"Shit, shit, shit." He threw the TV remote across the room, watching as it hit a potted plant and dirt scattered in all directions.

"Great," he groaned. "More shit to clean up. It can wait till tomorrow."

He sagged back again on the couch and closed his eyes.

The following morning, Eric got out of bed, determined to stop his pity party. He'd faced rough times before and this was nothing like that time.

He needed to get a grip.

His dreams hadn't been welcome, and had involved mixed and random occurrences, some of which had featured Kyle broken on the pavement. But Eric told himself that's all they were. Dreams. *His* Kyle was alive. Real.

After coffee, Eric sorted out some buttered toast then texted Kyle.

Soz bout lst nite. I wz shit comp. FanC a drink tonight?

Twenty minutes later—thinking he'd messed things up—he got a text back.

I have no idea what you said. Please translate. Queens English please. :)

Ha. The smiley face must mean Kyle wasn't mad. Instead of regaling Kyle with text slang, he called him. The phone rang five times before it was picked up.

"I hope this is Eric and not some snot-faced teenage skateboard dude. Honestly, I have no clue what half of that message said. All I recognised was the word drink." Kyle's tone was dry but there was a trace of wary amusement.

Eric snorted. "Sorry, I automatically assume everyone knows text slang. I said I'm sorry about last night. I was shit company and do you fancy a drink tonight?"

I can throw this mood off and make time for him. I need to. I miss him.

"Oh, I can't." Kyle said regretfully. "Luce leaves at midnight to go back to the US and we have a girls' night out. Just the two of us. Because no doubt there will be tears and snot. And plenty of drama when we wave goodbye." He snorted in amusement. "Plus Luce and

I have been tasked with getting something special organised for the club."

Eric tried to hide the disappointment in his voice. "Oh. She's off already? It was only last week we all had dinner together. Her departure came around quickly. Maybe another night then. I'll text her, say goodbye before she goes."

After what Luce had done for Kyle in Vegas, they deserved time together, and Eric certainly didn't begrudge them it.

There was silence, then Kyle spoke softly. "I heard that there's a great Impressionism exhibition at the National Gallery. Maybe you'd like to join me and we can go for dinner afterward? It's Monday night, so I guess you'll be off?"

Eric didn't have a clue what Impressionism meant but he wouldn't disappoint Kyle a second time.

"I like Impressionism." He made a mental note to look it up before they went out. "And Monday is good. And the best thing is it's only two days away. It's a date. Just let me know where to meet you."

"I'll do that. I'll text you but it won't be that stupid stuff you do." The smile in Kyle's voice warmed Eric. "Okay then, I'll speak to you soon. Looking forward to it."

Eric smiled at his phone. "Me too." He ended the call and slumped down into the armchair. His stomach was still queasy with the aftermath of yesterday's events.

Perhaps Aaron was right. Perhaps Eric needed to talk to someone again about the recurrence of the nightmares, the fact his job meant less and less to him each day and that he might have found someone else who was special.

Eric knew Kyle was important to him and was becoming more so every day. It was time to begin living again, to place his trust and caring in another person. Carrying the shadow of Lincoln's death in his soul and the still-twisted remnants of the similar event of yesterday was not going to bring him that solace.

With a sigh, Eric picked up his phone again and scrolled through the numbers. Then, with a resolve he drew up from his soul, he dialled a number he knew off by heart.

"Wow, that exhibition was amazing. The brushstrokes on that Cezanne were so intricate they were breath-taking." Kyle's enthusiasm about the art they'd seen should have lifted Eric's spirits more. Instead, he smiled and continued walking down the busy street, avoiding people coming in the opposite direction. The streets were packed, and he was irritated at the constant pushes and shoves as people strode past, uncaring of whether or not they knocked into anybody.

I should have known better than to go the therapist this morning. I should have cancelled. But Kyle was so looking forward to the exhibition.

This morning's session with his old doctor, Louisa Kenton, had been rough. A specialist in PTSD and survival guilt related disorders, she'd been soft-spoken yet thorough and it had left Eric feeling shattered and drained.

Dredging up old feelings had been tougher than he'd imagined. He'd never had thought his guilt at not saving Lincoln and surviving was a living thing, a despotic malingerer intent on destroying him from within. Dr Kenton had shown him a glimpse of the monster and Eric wasn't a fan. The fact he felt he'd failed at saving the suicide jumper hadn't helped either.

"I'm surprised you're so chipper when you got in at one this morning," Eric said dryly. "You sound as if you and Luce had a really good time."

Eric was glad that he'd managed to pull off normal. Sure, he'd been quiet—but then, Kyle said enough for both of them.

"Oh, we did," Kyle chirped. "We pub crawled, did the whole dance scene thing, then she caught her taxi to the airport around ten." His face clouded. "There was a lot of snot and drama. We were both a mess when we said goodbye, but she said she's coming back in six months' time." He bounced happily. "It's something to look forward to."

Eric frowned. "If she left at about ten, how come you got in at one?"

Kyle made puppy dog eyes at him. "I met up with an old friend. We had a few drinks afterward because I was still upset, and he was a shoulder to cry on."

"Anyone I know?" Eric asked. He felt a teeny bit put out Kyle hadn't called him, and yet, he'd been the one to tell him not to come over, hadn't he?

Kyle glanced at him slyly. "Maybe." He grinned widely. "Is that a hint of jealousy I detect there?"

Eric grunted. "No. I'm just being polite. You can be friends with whomever you want, you know that."

"Ooh, Mr Grumpy Pants," Kyle chided. He squeezed Eric's hand. "It was Ryan, you doofus. He'd dropped Mango off at the airport for some gung-ho conference he was going to and decided to pop in at the bar on his way home. That's where he saw me and we spent some time together."

Eric felt much better knowing it had been Ryan, but he wasn't going to give the satisfaction of letting Kyle know that. "I'm glad he's back to his old self now, and is getting out and about. That's cool."

"So, where do you want to go to get something to eat?" Kyle chattered beside him.

Eric glanced over and grinned. "Anywhere you like. What kind of cuisine do you fancy, my liege? The night is yours to command."

Kyle raised an eyebrow. "Oh, yeah? I can have anything I want?" He reached down and clasped Eric's hand tentatively. "This work?"

Eric's throat clogged up at the simple gesture. "That feels good." He squeezed Kyle's chilled hand harder.

The blinding smile Kyle gave him made Eric want to give him the world. *God, he's beautiful. I don't want to lose this—what we have. What we're building. I hope the feeling is mutual.*

"Hmm. Maybe we should try Korean? There's a great place a couple of blocks away," Kyle suggested.

"Sounds good. I don't think I've eaten Korean before. What's it like?"

As Kyle burbled on enthusiastically about tofu and kimchi, Eric's attention was diverted to an elderly man further away coming toward them with a guide dog. Eric deftly manoeuvred him and Kyle out of the way to allow him to pass unhindered.

Someone else, however, was not as courteous. A woman in front of them, carrying a shit ton of designer-labelled bags barrelled toward the man as if expecting him to give way. She was talking on a headset of some sort.

Eric opened his mouth to warn her to watch out. Before he could, the dog changed course, no doubt to attempt to change the owner's direction to avoid a collision. But the crowds were too thick and, as Eric watched in horror, the woman barrelled into the unseeing man, causing him to stagger and lose his balance.

He shouted in surprise and the dog gave a deep woof.

Leaving a startled Kyle behind him, Eric rushed forward to try and break the man's fall. He managed to grab an arm and used all his strength to curtail the man's descent. If he'd fallen to the pavement, the rushing throng of traffic may well have trampled on him.

"Sir, it's okay, I've got you. Here, let me help."

The man righted himself and threw a smile of gratitude toward Eric. "Thank you so much. I must have not been paying attention to Kirby..."

Eric presumed Kirby was the dog, who now sat patiently waiting for instructions.

"No," he said grimly, glaring at the woman who was clutching her parcels to her chest as if he were a thief attempting to take them from her. "It wasn't your fault. It was this woman who knocked you over. She was the one not watching where she was going." He stared at her. "Perhaps next time you could be more careful, madam."

"Fuck you," she spat, her face contorted with anger. "People like him shouldn't be allowed on the streets in rush hour. They're a bloody nuisance, them and their animals." Around them some curious eyes stared, but for the most part people scurried by uncaring.

A slow flare of temper crept through Eric's chest and he clenched his fists to keep it in check. "People like him," he said caustically. "You mean blind people? You're a nasty piece of work, aren't you?"

Kyle was at Eric's side now, a hand on his arm. "Calm down, babe." He moved over to the blind man. "Are you okay, sir? Can I help at all?"

"I'm good, young man." He waved a hand. "Thank you for asking though." He shook his head wearily. "And honestly, please don't get riled on my account. I'm used to it."

"Well, you shouldn't have to get used to it," Eric growled. "It's not right. You have as much right to be here with your dog as she has, selfish cow."

"Eric," Kyle said warningly. "Come on, let it go. She's not worth it."

The woman's eyes opened wider. "Not worth it? And what would you know about it, you freak?" She scrutinised Kyle, who stared back defiantly. "Fucking purple hair, piercings, and showing your body off. You're a sight, you are. I bet your mum's not proud of you, looking like that."

Kyle looked at her pityingly. "My mum's just fine with who I am, thanks. So am I."

Eric's fury welled at the bitch's biting words. In his opinion, Kyle looked perfect, and his tight stomach showing beneath the crop-top shirt he wore was fabulous.

His frustration at his therapy session and the emotions still surging beneath the surface got the better of him. "Better than being a bitch, lady. And leave my boyfriend alone. You want someone to insult, you can insult me."

Kyle pulled his arm, his face pale. "Eric, let's go. The gentleman is fine and there's no point causing a scene in public."

"I agree," the elderly man said. "Kirby and I need to get home to my wife. But thank you, both of you, for standing up for me. I appreciate it." He cast a glare in the direction of the now red-faced woman. "And you, madam, need to learn some manners. Good day."

With a farewell wave and Kirby leading the way, he set off. The woman harrumphed and turned to leave. But Eric couldn't let it go. "Enjoy the rest of your night," he called after her as she sashayed away. "Try not to knock any more elderly people down, why don't you?"

"Eric," Kyle hissed, face darkening. "That's enough. You're being a prick now."

Eric turned to Kyle in angry surprise. "A prick? For defending an old blind man? Jesus Christ, Kyle."

Kyle flinched. Eric moved toward him, arm out, intending on taking his hand to continue their walk home. His gut roiled at the sudden look of panic rising on Kyle's face. Kyle gathered his jacket closer around him in a defensive gesture and motioned to the street. "Let's go home. I've had enough of tonight." He moved swiftly forward, through the crowd. Eric followed, stricken at how the ending to their night had turned out.

Perhaps he had overreacted, but God, Kyle hadn't thought he was going to get violent with him, had he? Fuck it, surely, he knew him better than that?

Confused, awash with dread that he'd fucked up—again—and with the beginnings of a quiet flame of resentment that Kyle could even *think* that of him, Eric followed his lover home in silence.

Chapter Thirteen

Kyle opened the door to his flat and strode inside. He switched on the light and went to the kitchen for a glass of water. His hands were shaking slightly and he willed them still. Behind him, he heard Eric throw his jacket over the back of the couch and sit down in the armchair.

What the fuck had that all been about? He'd never seen Eric so aggressive, so in someone's face. It was as if the man he knew, the one who helped people and who had held him at night in some of the darkest of his times, was another person.

"Would you like a drink?"

Eric grunted, "No thanks."

Kyle turned back and poured another glass of water, downing it. He went over to the couch and sat down. Eric stared at him moodily.

"I'm sorry," he muttered. "For causing such a scene. I overreacted."

"Yes, you fucking did," Kyle retorted. "Care to tell me what had you in such a mood tonight? Don't think I couldn't see you were trying so hard to appear normal. I knew something was off the minute I saw you."

Eric shrugged. "It was a rough week. Not much to tell."

Kyle took a deep breath, trying to ignore the prickling irritation at Eric's reticence. *I spilt my guts and that's all I get?* "That's what *boyfriends* do, isn't it? Listen to your tales of woe?"

He hadn't missed the use of the word when Eric shouted it at the woman back on the street. At the time, it had given him a warm, fuzzy feeling that he'd been described that way.

Eric's nostrils flared at the word boyfriend.

"Unless of course, that was said in the heat of the moment and you didn't mean to use it." Kyle cocked an eyebrow.

Eric scowled. "I meant to use it. Duh. I mean, we are, aren't we?"

Even Kyle wasn't a hundred percent on that one, although he hoped so. "If you tell me what's bugging you. Otherwise, I'll have to recant the honorific." Kyle played his ace. "And you still owe me some payback, remember? A little something for me telling you my story. We agreed."

At that, something happened. Eric jumped to his feet and paced around the room like a caged animal.

"You want to see the inside of me? Try to figure me out and see if you can fix me? She tried that this morning and all it did was make me feel more miserable." He picked up a cushion and glared at it before flinging it back on the couch.

Kyle blinked. "Who tried what this morning? Who the fuck is *she*?"

The way Eric's arms folded across his chest told Kyle he wasn't happy about spilling the beans.

"I don't want to talk about it," he said. "It's my business."

Kyle had heard enough. "For fuck's sake. You just answered your own question about being boyfriends. If you're not ready to talk to me about whatever bug you have up your arse, I don't think that's a term we can call ourselves." His chest ached and his heart was bleeding but he had to say it. "I think the word fuckbuddies is more what you have in mind. And that's not something I want to be for you."

Eric remained silent and shut off. He folded his arms across his chest and looked down at the floor.

"The fact you aren't denying it makes me think it's the truth." The lump in Kyle's throat made the words hard. His eyes prickled but he was damned if he was going to cry. "Look, maybe we need to be alone tonight. You have issues. I have issues. Maybe this isn't a good idea right now." *Say something. Tell me I'm wrong and this is as serious for you as it is for me.*

Eric remained tight lipped. Kyle closed his eyes briefly then opened them to see Eric staring at him. His stormy gaze showed both pain and guilt but his face was unreadable.

Kyle reached for his phone. "I think maybe you should go home. I'll call you a taxi then we can see how things are tomorrow when we're both not so hyped up."

Eric stood up and pushed Kyle's hand away from the mobile. "That's not necessary," he said. "I'll find my own way home. Perhaps you're right. We need to think about things for a while. Alone."

Before Kyle could say anything, Eric had picked up his jacket and was out the door. It swung shut behind him and all Kyle could do was stand there and wonder how everything had suddenly turned to shit.

"And now—it's karaoke time!"

The audience in Club Delish roared in delight, anticipating the entertainment that was to come. Seated at the table in front of the stage, Kyle laughed out loud at how those words must have stricken fear and fury into Ryan. He knew how his boss felt about the dreaded curse of patrons butchering his favourite songs.

The fund-raising benefit had taken some organising; the little surprise they'd all planned for Ryan's unofficial welcome-back party had been hard to keep secret. Between himself, Luce, Mango and Lenny, though, they'd managed.

And now the object of that surprise, young teen singer and Goth sensation Callum Webster was pouring his heart out on stage. Kyle was sure when Ryan realised exactly who they'd convinced to karaoke at his club, all would be forgiven. His boss had an unholy crush on the singer. Luckily Kyle had an in with Callum from his days in Vegas and he'd been happy to oblige with a favour.

Kyle took another sip of his drink and looked around the room. He stared at the name badge on the table next to his, and wondered if Eric was still coming tonight. Since their argument a week ago, he hadn't heard a word from him.

He reflected drolly that it was just as well Eric had been out of the picture, as Kyle had had more time to devote to the event tonight. He was still hurt by the fact Eric hadn't even tried to get in touch.

And since Kyle had been left with plenty of time on his hands, he made sure his flat was sparkling and tidy. He tended to clean when he got upset.

"Penny for your thoughts?" Brook Hunter leaned across the table, his smile dazzling. Lenny's boyfriend, with his dark, debonair good looks, was a delicious specimen of man who wore a suit like a fashion model.

Kyle forced a grin. "Just thinking about Ryan's reaction when he heard the word 'karaoke.' I bet he threw a hissy fit the likes of which even Mango hasn't seen before."

Brook's hearty laugh rang out around the room. On stage, Laverne glanced their way and blew Brook a kiss.

"The lady is looking mighty fine tonight." Kyle waved a hand at Laverne. "She certainly knows how to put on a show."

"You know it," Brook said fondly as he regarded his partner. "And I wouldn't have it any other way for either of them."

"Evening."

Kyle's heart leapt at the familiar voice.

"Am I still welcome at the table?"

Kyle looked up. Eric looked splendid in a pair of dark blue smoothies and a pale blue shirt teamed with a trendy open waistcoat in differing shades of blue and grey. His auburn hair curled around his ears and Kyle noticed it had grown a little.

He shrugged. "Sure, feel free. It says your name right there." He felt a little better when Eric rolled his eyes at his sass as he sat down.

Brook nodded at him. "Hi Eric—you're looking good. How's things at work?"

Kyle tried not to listen to their conversation, affecting an air of disdain he didn't feel. He watched the show but kept his ears pricked for mentions of him or signs that Eric was missing him. They didn't come.

Why doesn't Eric look more upset that he hasn't seen me for a week? Why doesn't he talk to me, or apologise? Well, two can play that game.

For the rest of the evening, Kyle put on a great show of his card skills, amazing everyone with his dexterity. He chatted civilly to Eric, as if nothing had changed, and was gratified to see the confusion in his face that Kyle seemed unaffected by their parting.

Secretive bastard, Kyle thought savagely. See me not give a fuck. See me getting over you. And yet the whole time he was performing his famous croupier shuffling skills and showing his friends the magic tricks he'd learnt in Vegas at the side of the Great Hazzy Houzzini, Kyle was dying a little bit inside.

The 606 Club in Soho was one of Kyle's favourite jazz places. Intimate and bohemian, it was one of his go-to places when he needed cheering up. And cheering up was just what he needed.

It had been two days since he'd seen Eric at Club Delish, and since then he'd received one short message saying that it had been good to see him and Eric would be in touch soon. Kyle had responded back with a thumbs-up icon, and that had been as much as he could manage. So, when he sat in his favourite booth with a whisky sour—a drink of sheer perfection created by the legendary bartender Sergio—tapping his fingers to the strains of jazz floating across the room, the last thing he expected to see when he opened his eyes was Eric.

He looked tired; his eyes were shadowed, and he seemed thinner. He still looked good though, in ripped jeans and a white long-sleeved tee-shirt.

"Hey." Eric said, slipping his thumbs into his belt loops and leaning forward slightly.

"Hey, back." Kyle stared for a moment, and then realising it was getting them nowhere, he motioned to the seat beside him. "Want to sit down?"

Eric slid into the booth, the heat and touch of his body in the closed space instantly causing Kyle's groin to react.

"How did you know I was here?" Kyle asked then chuckled. "Don't tell me. Ryan."

Eric nodded. "He said you were coming down here tonight. That he'd given you the night off while he sees how Kellie does managing the club on her own." He frowned slightly. "She seems to be settling in well. Is everything okay there? Ryan's not thinking of replacing you or anything is he? Because you're one of the best things to happen to that club—"

Kyle reached over and pressed a firm finger over Eric's lips. "Don't be daft. I'm quite happy with having a bit more time off, to be honest. You know what my days off are usually like—popping down to check on things, catch up on paperwork I can't do when I'm there at night and do stock takes and shit. It's nice to not be the only one anymore. And Ryan would never do me wrong."

Eric didn't look convinced and Kyle's chest filled with warmth. *He's worried about my job. That's too sweet.*

"Well, okay. As long as you're happy."

Kyle decided the time had come to let Eric know exactly how he felt. It couldn't do any harm. After all, Eric had taken the time to seek him out, hadn't he? That must mean something.

"I haven't been happy for a while," he admitted, raising his glass and taking a sip while Eric beckoned a waitress over. "I missed you." *There, I said it. Deal with it.*

Instead of backing off as he half expected, Eric leaned over and fixed his eyes on Kyle's. They really are like peridot, he thought dreamily. So damn beautiful.

"I missed you too." Eric reached up and traced a warm finger along Kyle's cheekbone. "Like crazy. That's why I swung around tonight. To apologise and tell you I care about you and I'm not going to let you go over a stupid spat." He shrugged. "I had plenty of time to think about things and I think I'm in a better place to talk to you about it."

Kyle struggled to draw a breath after that admission. His insides were all tingly, and something else was getting happy too. Finally, he managed to respond.

"Glad to hear it," he murmured. "Maybe I should finish up my drink and we can go back to my place, finish what we started the other night?"

He gasped as Eric's hand reached under the table and squeezed his thigh. " Let me finish the drink I just ordered, watch this next set and then we can go. Deal?"

"Deal," Kyle agreed.

They sat in contemplative silence as the next band came on. Kyle's body swayed to the saxophone and drum work, and for a while, he lost himself in the rhythm.

Jazz, whisky and a sexy—and hopefully repentant—man beside him, willing to take whatever punishment Kyle offered.

Things were looking up.

They reached Kyle's house around eleven o'clock and he mixed them a drink. Eric looked around the flat with surprise.

"Your place is looking really tidy," he muttered as he took in the obsessively re-organised in alphabetical order DVD collection. His eyes drifted to Kyle's dice collection. "And you've added a few more of those."

Kyle looked over at his pride and joy fondly. He'd been acquiring dice for years and had quite the collection. "I had some time to hunt them out and buy a few more. Pretty cool, huh?"

"A few more?" Eric snorted in amusement. "You've bought a lot more than a few."

"Did you come here to talk about my dices—dice? Dicii? I never remember the plural for the damn things—or do you want to tell me what happened the other day that put you in such a bad mood?" Kyle plonked down beside Eric, making sure their legs touched.

The sigh Eric heaved seemed to have been dragged from deep inside. "I guess." He took a deep gulp of his drink and Kyle could see he was garnering courage for whatever he was about to tell him.

"That day we went to the gallery, I went to a therapist to talk about my 'problems.'" Eric used air quotes. "I knew I needed to talk to someone about it again given what happened the other day but..." He shook his head fiercely. "I wasn't prepared."

Kyle was mystified. "What the hell is 'it?' Are you being deliberately cryptic?"

Eric swung around to face him, eyes dark. "*It* was losing a man to suicide. The other day, when I was working a case, the guy jumped and I couldn't save him. It rehashed all the inadequacies and guilt I felt when I lost my partner in Nepal. I watched the man I loved fall to his death while saving me."

Kyle gasped in horror. "Eric, I'm so sorry. I can't even imagine—" He broke off as Eric made a cutting motion with his hand.

"It was the most unselfish and noble thing anyone has ever done for me. And I fucking hated him for it." The room fell silent. The bleak look in Eric's eyes spoke volumes and Kyle wasn't sure what to say.

Finally, he dragged up the courage to be the friend Eric had been a couple of weeks before when Kyle bared his soul. "Can you tell me what happened? I'd like to hear about it if you can tell me. You kind of scared me the other night." *So, this is what he's been hiding. God, he must have been devastated.*

A pang of fear, selfish but nonetheless real, took him by surprise. *Can I compete with a man who gave his life for his lover? How does anyone beat that? Especially me, who couldn't even stand up for himself with his psycho ex.*

It was the shuddering breath Eric took as he passed a hand over his eyes that made Kyle want to rush over and hug the life out of him. At least he was good for that.

After another minute of pacing, Eric sat down in his chair and closed his eyes. When he opened them, he stared at Kyle fiercely.

"First things first. You know I would *never* hurt you, right? I'm not a violent guy, and after what you went through, the idea of doing anything harmful to you appals me. The other night, I was on edge. No excuse, just…" He gazed at Kyle imploringly. "I'd never touch you in any way you didn't want."

Kyle rubbed his fingers along the top of Eric's hand. "I know," he said. "I do, honest. It's just sometimes, I get spooked."

"I'm sorry, babe," Eric said softly. "I never wanted to make you think of *him*. That's the last thing I ever want you to do. He's in your past, and let's hope he'll stay there."

He took a shuddering breath. "I guess I should start at the beginning. My boyfriend's name was Lincoln Dunbar. He was a couple of years older than me. I met him through a rock-climbing group. It used to be a thing of mine." He stopped, his face growing contemplative. "Linc was an experienced instructor and he taught me everything I knew about climbing. One thing led to another and we became a couple. I'd just joined the ambulance service so time together wasn't easy. But we managed. God, we managed."

A faint smile crossed his face at a memory and Kyle swallowed, feeling it was not becoming of him to be jealous of a dead man.

"In twenty-twelve, a group of us went to Nepal to do some climbing." Eric's face turned bleak. "We were on our way up to the summit of Everest when there was an earthquake." He looked down at his entwined hands in his lap. "It triggered an avalanche. Linc was bringing up the rear. My buddy Anton was at the top and Katherine was below me. We managed to swing into a cave. God knows how we managed it, but we did. Lincoln wasn't so lucky. The rope slipped, cut, fuck knows, and he went dangling off into the abyss." He halted, taking a deep, tortured breath.

Kyle's eyes stung as he fought to choke back tears at the distraught look on Eric's face. He couldn't speak for love or money, too caught up in the tragedy.

Eric continued, his voice rough. "I managed to pull him up, Anton was holding me, but he couldn't sustain it." He stood up, taking agitated strides around the room. "I told him, Aaron, don't you fucking let go of me. I'm going to pull Linc in." He gave a shuddering sigh. "And he tried, God he tried. But I kept slipping, going down the same way as Lincoln, while he kept telling me to leave him. But I couldn't. I had hold of his arm so tightly, but it was only his jacket and I—" he choked, tears running down his face. "Then he looked at me and said, "Time to save yourself. I love you, baby." And he let go. Just...let go."

Staring into space, seeing what had to be etched into him memory, he sputtered, "The bastard left me there holding his jacket and watching him fall into a fucking abyss." His face was ghastly pale and Kyle couldn't help the tears flowing freely down his face. His heart ached with pain and grieved for the man who'd given his life so Eric could live—and oh the tragedy for Eric to have seen it. Who wouldn't be traumatised by that experience?

This time, Kyle didn't care whether Eric wanted him close or not. Kyle needed to hold him.

"Oh, baby, I'm so sorry," he murmured helplessly as he pulled Eric into his chest and wrapped arms around him. Eric fell into him and his body shook with sobs.

"I hated him for leaving me," he stuttered, words muffled against Kyle's chest. "I put it behind me, tried to carry on. It was hard and I still miss him every day. But I was dealing with it, even with the nightmares, the memories. Then a few days ago, the day I blew you off, someone went and jumped off a building. I tried to stop him but I couldn't." He lifted his head and stared at Kyle with swollen eyes. "All I was left with was his damn cardigan. Just like before."

Kyle's heart broke in two right then. That Eric had been through this with someone he'd loved, and now, to bring it all to the fore again, a stranger had done the same. No wonder Eric was falling apart, and on the edge.

And it sounds like he still loves Lincoln.

Kyle swallowed, trying to relieve the ache in his throat at the thought Eric might not want him after all and he might have misjudged things.

"Let it out," he whispered against Eric's hair. "I'm here for you. No matter what the outcome is, I'll always be around."

Eric stilled then pulled free from Kyle's embrace. "What do you mean?" he choked out. "That sounds like you're planning on going somewhere." He sounded desperate.

"I'm not going anywhere," Kyle murmured. "Promise." *Not until you ask me to leave.*

Eric's face flooded with relief. "Oh, that's good. I thought..." His voice trailed off.

His face lighting up gave Kyle hope. "He sounds like a remarkable man, your Lincoln."

Eric nodded. "He was. We had good times together." He took Kyle's hand and rubbed his fingers gently across the top. Kyle watched the movement, mesmerised.

"When he died, I resented that I'd lived and he hadn't. Aaron calls it survivor's guilt. He says it's common enough." Eric traced circles on Kyle's palm. "Being in my current job doesn't help when I lose a patient. It's been worrying me a lot lately."

Kyle nodded. "I've read about that." He wrinkled his nose as he thought about the two of them. "I suppose you and I have that in common. We both survived something traumatic, although you lost someone dear to you and I didn't."

Eric chuckled weakly. "This isn't a competition, babe. When I think of the guy that hurt you that way, used you like a punching bag, did other foul things to you, I want to beat his lights out." He stopped and raised Kyle's hand to his lips, placing a soft kiss on his skin. "We both suffered, just in different ways."

Then bright green eyes looked into Kyle's. "So, I'm seeing my therapist again," Eric muttered. "She's helping me with some stuff."

Kyle wanted to laugh at the irony of it all. "That's good. I don't want to detract from your story, but"—he hesitated—"I am too. I finally caved in and am seeing someone about what happened to me in Vegas. Luce will be thrilled." He shrugged. "I understand what you're going through is what I'm trying to say."

Eric's eyes widened. "Wow, look at us. We're a truly modern couple, both in therapy and talking about our issues."

Kyle cleared his throat, not quite knowing how to phrase his next words. "Is this therapy bringing out old feelings? Are you, like…" he stuttered, "…discovering you still have unresolved feelings, anything I need to know about?"

"Are you asking me if I still love Lincoln?" Eric leaned forward and ran his finger along Kyle's bottom lip. "I'll always love him in my own way, in here." He touched his chest, and Kyle's throat went dry. "But he's not around now. I have plenty of room in my heart for someone else to love, and you fit perfectly. Like you were made for me."

Kyle's stomach fluttered and his body tingled as Eric face split into the most genuine smile Kyle had seen all day.

"Now kiss me, please. You have this habit of making me feel like nothing else matters. I need some of your Kyle magic right now."

The kiss that followed was like no other kiss Kyle had experienced. Eric's lips were a mix of salt and sweet, his hands clutching tightly to the back of Kyle's head, holding him there. Poignant and sweet, he didn't want to let go.

Being needed this way was a heady euphoria, and when the kiss changed from soft and subtle to deep, wet necessity, where tongues duelled and lips bit, there was no going back.

Standing as if they were one, the kiss went from one of support and compassion to a place where there were only two naked, desperate men, eager to touch and feel each other as if there would be no other chance to do so.

Eric manoeuvred them to the couch, his lips swollen with the force of their kisses, his beautiful body stretched out like a smorgasbord of something Kyle wanted to sample.

"I want you to make love to me," Eric whispered as he lay down, pulling Kyle on top of him. He opened his legs and beckoned Kyle in. "Need to be as close to you as I can get. You inside me…"

He reached his arms above his head, deliberately teasing Kyle. He resembled an infinitely sexier and debauched image of "Boy on the Bed" by Lucian Freud, another one of Kyle's favourite works of art.

"Oh, I'm happy to oblige," he said as he rubbed their cocks together, eliciting an appreciative moan from the man sprawled beneath him. He rummaged around under one of the cushions then produced the lube with a "Ta-dah." A condom was located too, and in record time, he was suited up and ready to go.

He watched, entranced, as Eric's fingers circled his own entrance, and couldn't hold back a moan when Eric plunged a finger inside himself, throat muscles straining.

"God, I could watch you do that all day." Kyle reached down and covered Eric's fingers with his own, slicking them with lube. "Now it's my turn."

He pushed Eric's legs up, gaining access to the enticing hole. He slid inside, watching Eric's mouth opening with a satisfied grunt. Emboldened, he thrust deeper, and this time, Eric groaned loudly and took firm hold of Kyle's arse, pulling him farther inside.

Heated flesh around Kyle's cock pulsed and gripped him, and he thought he'd lose his mind being so at one with a man he was falling in love with.

"God, baby, so good," Eric panted, eyes half shut, as he rutted upwards. "Fuck me harder."

"I thought we were calling this making love, not fucking," Kyle teased as he gained momentum and pounded into Eric's arse.

Eric's eyes flashed open dangerously. "I don't care what you want to call it," he said between gritted teeth. "All I know is that I want to come, and you doing exactly what you're doing right now is going to make that happen. Now shut the fuck up and get me off."

Kyle laughed and reached down to claim Eric's lips. He wasn't far off his own orgasm and knowing he could make a man come just by being inside him like this gave him a thrill of pride.

The slap of flesh against flesh and the silken slide of their sweat-sheened bodies was all Kyle needed. He came with a startled cry at the unexpected force of it, body tensing and hands gripping Eric's legs enough to make him growl with pain.

Eric's own release was impressive. Spurts of his spunk covered them both in sticky residue, the shockwaves of his climax taking hold of his body as he rode out the sensations.

At last, they lay still, supine and stuck together with come.

"That was something," Eric said drowsily. "You fucked my brains out."

Kyle smiled, his cheek stuck against his boyfriend's sticky chest hair. "You're welcome anytime."

He rolled off Eric reluctantly and stood, wincing at the rawness of his dick and the ache in his back where he'd probably pulled a muscle with his efforts.

"I think it's time to wash up and get into bed." He had a thought. "You know, we didn't even have any dinner." As if it heard him, his stomach rumbled. "I think I might make us something to eat then we can settle in."

Eric flapped a hand as he clambered off the couch. "Sure. I'll go take a pee and clean up. I'll come give you a hand in a minute."

Kyle was already planning what he was going to cook as he walked into the kitchen. "No problem."

Half an hour later there was no sign of Eric but there were two plates of carbonara pasta on a plate, with two glasses of wine. Kyle wandered into the bedroom and stood still.

Eric was face down on the bed covers, naked and snoring heavily. Kyle took a moment to enjoy the sight before he laid the tray on the chest of drawers.

"Nice," he muttered. "I slave away in the kitchen and you come in here and take over my bed. Huh."

He pulled the extra duvet from the cupboard, not wanting to roll Eric over and disturb him. Then he covered him with it and crawled into bed. He made sure to bring his pasta and wine with him.

"You might not want this, but I'm bloody starving." Kyle leaned down and kissed Eric's cheek. "Sleep tight, babe." He hesitated then whispered, "I'm falling hard for you, you know that?"

He didn't think he was at any risk of Eric hearing. His man was out for the count.

Chapter Fourteen

Eric clapped his hands over his ears at the caterwauling coming from inside of the truck. Great partner Aaron may be, but singer, he was not. And hearing "It's Raining Men" sung in his off-key tones caused Eric's arse to clench and his ears to bleed.

"You're killing me," he complained as Aaron hit a particularly high note. "Can you not do that please? I think you just pierced my eardrum."

"I don't think so," Aaron sang along with the lines. "Hallelujah, I don't think so, amen."

Eric reached out and switched the radio off. Aaron looked at him, an injured expression on his face.

"Hey," he protested. "I was just getting to the good bit."

"There are no good bits," Eric grumbled as he fiddled with the paperwork on his lap. "Only *really* bad bits."

Aaron huffed and waved a hand dramatically. "I was bringing out my inner queen," he stated. "Leah said I was in touch with my feminine side the other night, so I decided to enjoy it a little bit more. Heathen."

"Yeah, yeah." Eric grinned as Dispatch crackled into sound. "I think I prefer your man side when it comes to your singing."

The radio operator announced a new call and Eric frowned.

"Isn't that the same address we attended a while ago? The nutty lady who pulled a knife on us, with the mom and kids?"

"Yeah." Aaron's face was grim. "Sounds like something's gone down there again. Maybe this time she's gone too far." He looked at Eric. "Should we call in for police backup?"

They stared at each other for a minute then both shook their heads at the same time.

"Nah," Aaron said. "The police are busy enough as it is. I'm sure we can manage one crazy lady between us now we know what to watch out for."

Eric nodded in agreement. They drove in silence then Eric looked at his partner. "So, you and Leah still going strong? I bet your bubbie is happy."

Aaron smiled, a wide beam that split his face. "Yeah, Leah's great. She and my gran get on well, and now bubbie is even bossier than before, which I didn't think was humanly possible." He smiled wryly. "'Cut your hair; you'd look more handsome for her. Don't forget to take that lovely flower arrangement home with you for Leah—she'll love it. When is the wedding day? You don't want to lose that one, she's a keeper—'" He rolled his eyes. "Two strong women in my life is more than I bargained for."

From the beatific look on his face, Aaron didn't seem too worried about that, Eric thought.

"So how are you and Kyle getting on? It's been, what, over three months now you've been dating? You practically live at his place. When are you two moving in together?"

Eric grinned. "Too soon for that. But, yeah, I do spend a lot of time at his place since it's closer to the club. Our work rotas are a bitch to try and get time together."

Aaron peered at him. "With that grin on your face, mate, I'd say the two of you are coping well enough. I'm glad you got over your little spat. You were an insufferable bastard when the two of you were arguing."

Eric opened his mouth to deny it then closed it. Aaron was right; he had been a moody git at the time. But that had been nearly two months ago. They had now reached a level of what Kyle laughingly called "boyfriendship" they both were comfortable with.

Toothbrushes at each other's homes, spare clothes in the closet, microwave popcorn for Kyle in Eric's cupboards and bags of crisps for Eric in Kyle's—these were all signs of their rapidly evolving relationship.

Friends, lovers, partners—whatever you wanted to call it, Eric was glad it had happened. He couldn't imagine a life without his purple-haired, vivacious and sexy boyfriend. He had a feeling Kyle felt the same but neither of them had really committed to the L-word yet. Like Kyle—who was quick, quirky and full of depth—Eric's emotions had grown the same way.

"Get that soppy look off your face, you lovesick sap. We're here." Aaron stopped outside the house they'd been to before.

Eric blinked himself back to reality and looked around. He sighed. They were once again in a tough part of the city and they needed to be wary. And last time they'd been threatened. This call was not going to be a walk in the park.

They picked up their bags and approached the house. All the radio operator had said was another potential heart attack victim needing assistance.

Eric knocked on the door. There was no response. He knocked again.

This time the door opened and the same woman who'd held a knife on them last time stood there. Eric was pleased to note this time she had nothing in her hand except a ragged dishcloth. Sunglasses covered her eyes.

"Thank God you're here," the woman said. "It's my mum again. She's not well."

Jessie, Eric thought suddenly. Her name was Jessie. He smiled at her as he and his partner brushed past the narrow doorway into the dingy living room.

"Can you tell us what happened, Jessie? Did she have another heart—?"

He stopped short, Aaron swearing as he bumped into him. "Damn, Eric, warn me next time, will you?"

Eric's sarcastic reply was choked off, his throat going dry as he observed the scene before him. The older woman—Jessie's mother, he guessed—lay in a pool of blood on the carpet, eyes unstaring, her head a mess of blood, tissue and bone. Next to her was a large brick covered in gore.

"Aaron, this isn't a fucking heart attack. Call in backup. We need the police for this one." He moved swiftly to the woman's side, but from the mess her skull was in, he knew she was dead.

Obviously not hearing him, Aaron barrelled into the room, crouching beside him and feeling for a pulse. He looked up, his dark eyes meeting Eric's. The two of them swivelled their heads around to see a smirking Jessie standing above them. Her sunglasses had gone, but in her left hand was a large kitchen knife.

Fear tingled its way down Eric's spine.

Shit, not again. This woman is insane. She's also as high as a kite.

As if pulled by an invisible puppeteer's string, both men stood together and faced the unstable woman before them.

"I told you," Jessie hissed as she blocked the doorway. "I told *her*"—she motioned with the knife to the dead woman on the floor—"what would happen if I didn't get my kids back. Now those fuckers at DSS have decided to keep them. I warned you all I wouldn't be happy."

"Jessie, we've been in this place before," Eric said softly. "Put the knife down and let's talk."

Jessie cackled loudly, eyes dilated and spittle in the corners of her mouth. "Talk? It was you talking that got me into this mess, you wanker. You told them Social Services bitches about me and they took my kids away. I never got no money no more. Then she—" She gave one savage gesture at the woman on the floor. "She had the fuckin' cheek to tell them she didn't think it was a good idea to give 'em back to me." Her eyes narrowed and a smirk crossed her face. "But I showed her. I bricked her one and she fucking stopped talking, didn't she?" She nodded. "Yeah, I showed the mummy bitch who was boss."

Eric's gorge rose at the sheer malevolence in her voice. Beside him Aaron moved, and the knife moved his way threateningly.

"You need help, Jessie," Aaron said, his voice soothing. "We can do that. Give you something to calm you down, get you to a hospital so they can look after you. Wouldn't you like that—someone looking after you, not worrying about bills or cleaning up this mess?"

Jessie tilted her head to one side, considering his suggestions. "What, three shitty meals a day, wipe my bum, put me in fucking prison care? I'm better off here, turning tricks. At least those blokes give me a good dinner now and then. That's what you made me do, you know? Fuck people for money. Because you took away my income."

Eric was pretty sure that had been what Jessie had been doing as a living even before their first call out.

Not going to argue with the crazy bitch with a knife. We need her to surrender it.

He moved forward, Aaron's hissed "Eric, no." ringing in his ears. Outside, he heard sirens.

"Jessie, come on. Let go of the knife, and we'll sit and have a talk, 'kay? I've got something in my bag I can give you to help you come down from wherever you are. Then we can get someone in to take your mum away, so she has some dignity. Come on. Let us help you. Please."

Jessie's lips thinned and she looked from him to Aaron. Finally, she looked down at the body on the floor and a faint expression of fear crossed her face.

Eric held his breath as he waited for her answer. Finally, she nodded and the knifepoint slowly descended down.

"Just drop the knife on the floor," Eric said as he moved toward her warily. Aaron made a sound behind him but Eric ignored it. The knife fell harmlessly to the floor and Eric let out a breath of relief as he reached her.

"Great, now let's sit down and—"

At first, the sharp pain in his left side didn't register. It was only a split second of agony followed by a sudden breathlessness as the shock of being stabbed hit him. He reeled backward, hearing Aaron's agonised cry and Jessie's peal of cruel laughter.

She must have had another knife somewhere. Shit, I need to see what the damage is. I hope she didn't hit an artery. His paramedic mind in full throttle despite the pain, Eric staggered backward, wondering why the room was growing dim and fuzzy, his eyes losing focus. Between his fingers, copious amounts of blood seeped in puddles onto an already blood-spattered floor.

He was aware of someone bending over him—not Aaron, another uniformed man. He tried to keep his eyes open, see if Aaron was safe, but it was just too much.

His last thought before he succumbed to unconsciousness was of violet eyes and a warm smile.

"Hey, baby. I'm not sure if you can hear me. The nurse says you can, so I hope so. You're doing okay. The doctor says the knife hit a blood vessel, but Aaron got you all fixed up quickly. I guess that's the one benefit of having a paramedic and a truck on call, right? Anyway, Aaron said to tell you he's fine and he needs his partner back because the one he's got now is driving him fucking crazy."

There was a soft giggle followed by a sniffle. "That's his words, not mine." There was the sound of rustling. "I bought you some grapes, because everyone knows that's what you bring to a hospital, right? And I also got you a beautiful bunch of flowers, only the hospital wouldn't let me bring it in because apparently, it's not healthy. And the sister on the ward didn't stop sneezing. It's a pity 'cause I chose them myself and did the arrangement. I had to take them home again." Kyle sounded terribly peeved.

Eric tried to laugh but it was too painful. He felt as if he'd gone three rounds with a heavyweight boxer. But the insane boyfriend babbling was adorable and he wanted to kiss him.

"Oh my God, you can hear me? Eric, open your eyes, love. Please open your eyes." The desperation in Kyle's voice energised Eric into finally doing what he was told. The first sight that greeted him was Kyle's face, anxious and pale, with red-rimmed eyes. Eric had never seen anything more welcoming.

"Hi," he croaked, throat burning. His eyes watered with the bright light of the room. "I'm glad you're here."

Kyle loomed over him, fussing with his pillows to raise his head up. "Where else would I be?" he asked waspishly. "You decided to go and get yourself stabbed. This is generally where those people end up, with the people who love them worrying over them."

Despite the snark in the comment, Eric heard the vulnerability beneath. And the roundabout declaration of love that made his heart race.

"Come here," he instructed, raising one arm carefully so as not to dislodge whatever drips were in it. "I need to hold you. Just be careful. I have been in the wars with a knife-wielding maniac."

Kyle leaned down and buried his face in Eric's neck so close it was as if they were joined by damp skin. "I thought I'd lost you, you bastard," he whispered tremulously against Eric's skin. "I was so worried about you."

Eric gave him a one-armed hug, as strong as he could manage. "I'm here," he murmured, stroking Kyle's hair. "You think I'd go anywhere without you?"

"Well, okay," Kyle retorted, his words muffled. "I wouldn't want to have followed you down there." He waved a hand at the floor. "But I'm good with anywhere else."

Eric grinned. "What makes you think I would have gone to Hell?" he said teasingly.

Kyle looked up, a smile in his eyes. "Duh, don't all sexy bad boys go there? I think it's the law." He cupped Eric's face in cool hands. "God, when they told me you were here, I didn't know what to do. Ryan kicked me out of the club, told me to stay here until I was sure you were okay."

"So how long have I been out? And what happened from the time I hit the deck?" Eric shifted uncomfortably. His whole body ached and his left side burnt like hell.

"Two days. They brought you in on Wednesday. Today's Friday afternoon." Kyle scowled. "The crazy bitch that stabbed you was taken down by the police who'd already been on route. She had another knife on standby it looked like, hidden on the mantelpiece." He scowled. "What is it with people and knives in this country? Anyway, the poor old lady screaming on the phone to Social Services as her head was bashed in generated some warning bells." He grimaced. "They called the coppers and they arrived in time to save your arses. Aaron did his magic and you were rushed into surgery. And poof, here you are."

Eric leaned back on his pillows, exhausted. "I'm going to be okay then? Nothing vital damaged?"

Kyle nodded. "The doctor says you'll be fine. Just need rest, and a lot of sex."

Eric gaped. "What?"

Kyle's face was mischievous. "Oh, yeah, he said I was the cutest guy he'd ever seen and as long as I gave you loads of love and sex, your recovery was guaranteed. I couldn't let the best advice of the medical profession go to waste so I wrote down a plan, see?" He held up a calendar with red crosses all over it. Hardly any of the page could be seen.

He pointed at one line. "This is where we have butt sex, me on the bottom. This one," he dragged his finger along, "is sixty-nine sex. This one here is a blowjob for you, and here again we have—butt sex. You on the bottom this time. I have your medical recovery programme all planned out." He looked pleased with himself and Eric choked as he laughed.

"*This* is what you've been doing while I've been lying here unconscious? Did you perhaps do anything more personal while I was out?" He lifted his covers with difficulty. "I look as if I'm intact. No cock cage or anal beads up my arse. I think."

Kyle reached over and pressed warm lips to his. "I might have peeked now and then, just to see you were still functioning." He chuckled against Eric's mouth.

"God, you are so crazy, but I love you." Eric yawned, wondering why Kyle's eyes widened and his mouth dropped. He was also becoming dizzy and floaty.

"Do you think you could ask the nurse if I could have some water or something? I'm parched." His voice sounded slurred and he frowned.

Perhaps he should go to sleep for a bit. After he had his water.

"Yeah, sure," Kyle stammered. "I'll, erm, go fetch her." He scuttled out of the room as if all the demons from hell were at his heels.

Closing his eyes, Eric imagined he and Kyle were on a soft, white beach somewhere, with cocktails. Kyle was in a tiny, dark blue Speedo and had never looked so delicious. His body was tanned and toned, his arse framed by the tight trunks and all Eric wanted to do was throw him down on the sand and…

"He looks weird, like he's dreaming." Kyle's whisper made him come back to the present. "Is it the drugs you're giving him?"

There was a soft laugh. "Dearie, he's on so much medication I'm surprised he's awake and lucid. It must be you he came back for from the deep, dark doldrums. He's a tough bugger, this one."

Eric's eyes remained closed because they were heavy and he couldn't bother opening them right now. *Yep, you're the one that I want, Kyle baby. Only you…*

"Oh, so he might not be saying things he'll remember later, when he's not on the meds?" Kyle sounded disappointed.

"I think the medicine has just caught up with him now, that's all. He's been through a lot, what with the surgery. I'm sure whatever he said to you meant something to him at the time."

What did I say to him? Oh, yeah, I think I told him I love him.

Eric tried to nod to assure Kyle that, yes, indeed, he'd meant every word and he'd tell him again when he was up and about just in case he needed to hear it again.

The nod seemed to grow heavier and Eric surrendered to the warmth of the darkness of sleep calling his name.

"I'm not an invalid. I can make it on my own," Eric grumbled as Kyle helped him out of the car. Little Lady *was* tough to get out of when you were still stitched up and sore, but he was determined he could get out of his Roadster without help.

Kyle dangled the car keys in front of him. "Says the man who insisted he could drive us here then ended up having a mini stroke when he pushed down on the pedals." He slammed the door shut and beamed at his boyfriend. "Lucky I was there to help out. She's awesome to drive."

"Yeah, well, don't get used to it," Eric said.

Kyle sniggered. "God, you are such a grump. Come here. Perhaps this will make you feel better."

In full view of the neighbours outside Aaron's bubbie's house, Kyle drew him close and kissed him thoroughly. When he finally let go, Eric was breathless, hard and feeling better. Kyle's kisses should have been declared a natural amphetamine the way they made his heart beat so fast.

"Tell me again what this visit is in aid of?" Kyle reached into the back of the car and took out a bottle of wine and a bouquet of flowers. "I remember you said something about meeting Aaron's girlfriend. Is this his house?"

Eric bit back a laugh. "Nope." He walked slowly up the path towards the small, terraced house in the middle of Islington. His side still hurt but he was a lot better than he'd been three weeks ago.

Kyle's tender ministrations, some great medical care and a lot of rest had got him back on his feet quicker than anyone had expected. Kyle still swore it was due to the gentle, yet exhilarating sex sessions prescribed on his calendar.

His boyfriend caught up with him. "Oh, so it's her house?"

"Nope." Eric smiled to himself at Kyle's exasperated grumble behind him.

"Why do you have to be so damned secretive? What is it with you?" He swatted away a bumblebee and scowled.

Eric knocked on the door. *You'll soon find out. Welcome to your baptism of fire.*

The door opened to reveal a tiny sprite of a woman with jet-black hair streaked with silver-grey and a myriad of coloured baubles around her neck, dangling across her flat chest. She was dressed in multi-coloured paisley trousers and wore a bright orange blouse, stained with something Eric wasn't sure about.

"Shalom, Eric, my boy. It's been ages since I've seen you. You look a bit pale. Are you eating properly since your accident?" Shrewd pale blue eyes turned to assess Kyle. "Is this the mensch Aaron told me about? Oy vay, he's skinny. And what's with all that metal in that pretty face?" She shook her head. "I'll never understand it."

Eric stifled a laugh at Kyle's gobsmacked expression.

"Bubbie Norma, it's good to see you again. And yes, this mensch is my boyfriend, Kyle."

Norma waved them in. "Come in, don't stand there on the doorway. The neighbours will think I'm having a sex party."

Kyle's jaw dropped even further. He was speechless for the first time since Eric had known him. *Mission accomplished. Thank you, Norma.*

As Norma propelled Kyle into a small lounge, his wide eyes stared back at Eric in panic.

"Come, sit," she fussed as she pushed Kyle physically down into an armchair covered with varying degrees of what looked like knotted multi-coloured cords. She swept them onto the floor with an impatient flip of her hand and turned back to Eric.

"Tea? Aaron and Leah will be here in a while. They walked to the shop to get me some more milk, although I'm sure they've taken the opportunity to make out somewhere along the way. They've been gone a while."

She motioned to the chair full of ropes. "Chuck that on the floor if you need room—it's only my macramé project for the local Women's Institute."

"Tea would be good, thank you. We'll sit and wait for Aaron." Eric smiled at Norma who gave him a beaming smile and scurried off into the kitchen.

Kyle was up in a shot, standing in front of Eric. "What the hell? You didn't warn me some crazy Yiddish grandmother was going to accost me. I'm assuming that's Aaron's bubbie." He glanced uneasily toward the kitchen. "I mean, she seems nice enough but she gets a bit personal, doesn't she?" He fingered his eyebrow stud nervously then his fingers drifted to the one in his lip. He'd finally taken the plunge and had it done. "Should I have taken these out to visit? I would have if I'd known—"

Eric silenced him with a swift kiss. "No, never. I love you just the way you are, so I'd never ask you to remove anything that makes you, you."

Kyle looked down at the floor. "That's the second time you've said that to me," he muttered. "I'll be starting to think you mean it soon." His violet eyes flashed with emotion and Eric choked back the words that sprung to his lips.

No, not yet. You have a plan, remember? Stick to the plan or Aaron will kill you. He spent hours shopping with you for the right thing. His hand drifted to his pocket, and satisfied the item was still there he gave a sigh of relief.

"Yes, that's her. She's quite the character. And, as you can tell, forthright. She's amazing though."

He didn't miss the disappointment on Kyle's face. They hadn't really talked about their expressions of loving each other since the accident. It had been a time devoted to healing and recovery, but Eric was damned sure that was going to change tonight, with his close friend and a woman he counted as a surrogate mother.

Ten minutes later, Aaron arrived with a pretty, dark-haired woman he introduced as his girlfriend, Leah. She was tall, curvy and had short, spiky hair that suited her round face. Eric could see the couple were besotted with each other.

They all sat down while Norma forced slices of cake, homemade rugelach and copious amounts of tea upon them.

Eric sat next to Kyle, his hand loosely resting on his thigh.

"So, my Eric, what happened to that bad woman who stabbed you? And her poor mother. Oy." Norma fanned herself. "What a terrible thing to happen."

"She was admitted to hospital and is undergoing psychiatric evaluation," Eric said. "We'll have to see what happens when they finish with that."

"Well, I hope they lock her up forever," Kyle spat out fiercely. "She deserves to go to prison for what she did. Bashing the poor woman's brains in and nearly killing you."

Norma laughed. "You have a little spitfire there, Eric. I like him already. So, when is the—"

Aaron cut her off with a glare and a wave of his hand. "Cut it out, bubbie. Don't even ask that question."

Leah giggled beside him and he took her hand. "And don't start on us either. I told you, when we're ready, we're ready."

Norma sat back and folded her arms across her chest. She pouted. "You don't let me have any fun, do you? I have a yen to plan a wedding. Someone get married, please."

Her eyes glinted as she leaned in toward Kyle. He made an instinctive movement back. She raised one finger and waggled it at him.

"A little bird told me—"

"Bubbie, could you please fetch the stuff from the kitchen? You know—the stuff we need to do the thing?" Aaron's voice was desperate. He shot an apologetic glance at Eric, who was having trouble breathing with the need to laugh and the knowledge of what he was about to do.

"The thing? What thing?" Norma looked confused. Then, as Aaron's glare grew fiercer, she nodded slowly. "Oh, *that* thing. My wish is your command, grandson. I am but a slave here to do your bidding." Muttering under her breath, she disappeared once again into the kitchen.

Eric swallowed down his nervousness and turned to Kyle, who looked like a hare caught in headlights. "What's going on?" he asked dazedly. "I swear I feel like I've stepped into the Twilight Zone. Have I missed something?"

"No, baby." Eric shuffled closer to Kyle and reached up to draw a hand through the spiky hair. "I have something to tell you and I wanted to do it with my friend and his crazy grandmother present."

Kyle looked visibly nervous. "Oh, wow. Way to pressure a guy. That sounds ominous." He fiddled with his lip ring again.

Norma came in bearing flute glasses and a bottle of champagne. She set them down and then settled in her armchair again, cherubic smile on her face.

"Go on," she commanded to Eric. "Do it."

"Oh, God," Kyle said faintly. His lip ring twiddling got worse.

Eric reached out and took his hand away from his mouth. "I said something to you when I was in the hospital. Something I meant then and I mean now. Do you remember what I said? You were worried I'd forget about it."

Kyle nodded. "Yeah, I remember."

"What did I say to you?" Eric prompted.

Kyle stared around at the faces watching him and closed his eyes momentarily. When he opened them, they were shiny. "That you loved me."

Eric reached out and caressed Kyle's face tenderly. "I love you. It wasn't the drugs talking, it was all me. Being there, knowing I might not have made it—I needed you to know that."

He reached into his pocket and grinned at the panic on Kyle's face. "Don't worry. Despite bubbie's need to have a wedding, I'm not going to ask you to marry me. Yet."

Kyle's shoulders sagged in relief but he stared at Eric, entranced, as he continued speaking. "We both know it's too soon for that."

Norma made a noise like a fart. Eric ignored her and removed a small velvet bag from his pocket. He reached in and drew out one of the two platinum bracelets he'd had made.

"They're commitment bracelets. Yours says 'I'm His' and mine says 'I'm Yours.' Or we can swap them around if you fancy a change." He chuckled. "Either way, it means I want you by my side as long as you'll have me."

Kyle's eyes were wet with tears as he nodded. "I love you too. And I'm not fussy about what mine says. Either way, it's true."

Heart full, Eric took Kyle's slim wrist and slid the "I'm His" bracelet over, rubbing at the soft skin with his thumb. Then, among soft claps from Aaron and Leah, and a series of noisy hoots interspersed with Yiddish gibberish Eric couldn't even hope to understand, Eric kissed his man.

As they sat drinking their celebratory champagne, Eric's mobile rang. He mouthed at Kyle—"Deacon"—then whispered, "Did I tell you we were all meeting them for dinner tonight so they can say congratulations?"

Kyle shook his head, smiling. "No, babe, you didn't. You're just full of surprises today, aren't you? Sounds good though." He and Eric'd had dinner with Deacon and his wife Chrissy a couple of times, and he'd found Deacon to be a real character. In a way, he felt sorry for Chrissy and Eric, what with Deke's hare-brained enthusiasm for get-rich-quick schemes.

"Hey, Deke, what's up?" Eric's grin grew wider as he listened. "Buddy, I'm not sure that's a good idea." His shoulders shook with laughter. "I get the whole concept, but hanging your baby up on a wall or a door so you have your hands free sounds like a pretty radical idea. Isn't that what those baby knapsack thingies are for?"

Kyle's jaw dropped. He mouthed, "What the hell?" at Eric who was struggling to contain himself. Everyone else was laughing too.

"Deke, hang on, Kyle wants to ask you about your idea—he's dying to find out what it's all about." With a wicked grin, Eric thrust his phone into Kyle's hand, and he stared mystified at his boyfriend, who had tears rolling down his cheeks.

Kyle sighed and raised the phone to his ear. "Hey, Deke."

"My man, Kyle. Please tell my wife and my stupid, ignorant friend that a baby carrier that you can hang on a wall, or a door or in a tree, is a great idea. You could, like, push him as well, like a swing if you hung it in a tree, have a bit of fun too." Deacon's voice became higher with enthusiasm. "It gives the parents their hands back and the baby can just hang around until they're done. You know, like in a bathroom when you need to wash your hands or do your business. You hang baby up with this device, like a strap that you can carry him around in on your body but adapts to hang up elsewhere. A bit like a sturdy coat-hanger that goes over the door."

Kyle blinked. "What does, err, Chrissy think about this?"

Deacon snorted. "Please, she thinks people will end up forgetting the baby and walking out of the bathroom leaving him hanging, or that the tree branch might break, or that the baby will break free and fall down or something. I mean, as a parent, you'd make sure the kid was safe, right? And you'd never forget your baby in a bloody bathroom. As if. What do you think?"

Kyle walked over toward Eric. "I think it's a great idea."

Aaron hooted with laughter and Norma gave a smile of satisfaction. "That'll teach you to put Kyle on the spot like that," she smirked.

Eric's head shot up and he stared at Kyle in horror. He smirked. "In fact, Eric agrees with me. He's even got a name for it. The Kiddy Keeper. Here. I'll hand him back over so you two can discuss it more. Oh, and I believe we're seeing you for dinner later. I look forward to it."

With a snigger, Kyle handed the phone back to Eric, who glared daggers. Aaron, Leah and Norma chuckled as they looked on.

Kyle slapped palms with the others in triumph as Eric tried to convince his best friend that, no, he didn't think the Kiddy Keeper was a good idea after all.

Later, lying at home after a slow, steamy session of lovemaking, Eric decided it was time to tell Kyle his other bit of good news.

"I have something else to tell you." He *oomphed* as Kyle moved on top of him, straddling his hips. His arse was still slick from Eric's come. They'd dispensed with condoms weeks ago. Eric was tested in the hospital as a matter of course, and Kyle decided to get it done then too.

"More to tell me?" He wiggled his bum suggestively against Eric's rapidly rising dick. "Is it my birthday or something that I'm being spoilt?" He squinted down at Eric. "It's good news, right? I don't want bad news when I'm on a high."

"It's good news to me." Eric lifted his arms and laid them above his head, stretching out. "I'm leaving the ambulance service."

Kyle's sexy movements stopped. "What? Since when? Why?"

"You know I've been burning out in this job. My heart isn't in it anymore. I applied for a job as an advanced paramedic practitioner for a large GP practice. I got it."

Kyle leaned down and placed a soft kiss on Eric's cheek. "What does that mean for you?"

Eric reached up and drew Kyle down to lie flat on his chest and nuzzled his neck. "It means I get to see you more often. I won't be working crazy shifts. It will still be damned hard work and I'll have some further studying to do, but I'm happy with it. I think I'll fit in there. The people seem really nice."

Kyle sighed. "Have you told Aaron yet? He's going to be mad."

Eric nodded. "Yes, he knows. I needed his advice about the new job. He's not happy. But he understands. He knows you're more important now."

Kyle sat up, hands splayed on Eric's chest. "Then I approve. Whatever makes you happy, babe. That's all I want." He gave a wicked grin and wrapped his hand around Eric's cock. "And this. This makes me happy too."

Wet, warm lips found Eric's, and as Kyle proceeded to ride him into oblivion, Eric thought dreamily he couldn't have wished for a better way to finish his day.

AUTHOR NOTE

Any assumptions or errors in this book about the life of a paramedic, the procedures they use, the ambulance service or the way Las Vegas casinos are run, are my own and may have been adapted for fictional purposes.

ABOUT THE AUTHOR

Susan Mac Nicol is a self-confessed bookaholic, an avid watcher of videos of sexy pole-dancing men, a self-confessed geek and nerd, and in love with her Smartphone. This little treasure is called 'the boyfriend' by her long suffering husband, who says if it vibrated there'd be no need for him. Susan hasn't had the heart to tell him there's an app for that.

A lover of walks in the forest, theatre productions, dabbling her toes in the cold North Sea and the vibrant city of London where you can experience all four seasons in a day, she is a hater of pantomime (please don't tar and feather her), duplicitous people, bigotry and self-righteous idiots. She likes to think of herself as a 'half full' kind of gal, although sometimes that philosophy is sorely tested.

In an ideal world, Susan Mac Nicol would be Queen of England and banish all the bad people to the Never Never Lands of Wherever-Who Cares. As that's not going to happen, she contents herself with writing her HEA stories and pretending that, just for a little while, good things happen to good people.

CONNECT WITH SUSAN

Interested in reading more of my books featuring men who make you swoon, steamy scenes and an engrossing relationship story? If you sign up for my newsletter at www.susanmacnicol.net, I'll send you a complimentary copy of one of my standalone titles, or perhaps the first book in my Men of London series, **Love You Senseless**. I don't do too many newsletters, so it's a low volume list. You have no obligation to buy anything, and you can of course unsubscribe at any time.

Did you enjoy this book? Drop us a line and say so! We love to hear from readers, and so do our authors. To connect, visit www.boroughspublishinggroup.com online, send comments directly to info@boroughspublishinggroup.com, or friend us on Facebook and Twitter. And be sure to check back regularly for contests and new releases in your favorite subgenres of romance!

Are you an aspiring writer? Check out www.boroughspublishinggroup.com/submit and see if we can help you make your dreams come true.

Made in the USA
Columbia, SC
26 February 2022